# DEFENDER OF THE FAITH

## Also by Sara Swann

House of Madness
Katie's Plain Regret
As it Pleases the King
Back from the Dead Red

# DEFENDER
## OF THE
# FAITH

Drăculești Dynasty
Book 1

# SARA SWANN

WordCrafts

Although a work of fiction, ***Defender of the Faith*** is based on actual events. The author has endeavored to be respectful to all persons, places, and events presented in this novel, and attempted to be as accurate as possible. Still, this is a novel, and all references to persons, places, and events are fictitious or used fictitiously.

Scripture quotations taken from The Holy Bible, New International Version® NIV® Copyright © 1973, 1978, 1984, 2011 by Biblica, Inc. Used with permission. All rights reserved worldwide.

*Defender of the Faith*
Copyright © 2024
Sara Swann

ISBN: 978-1-962218-56-6

Cover concept and design by Mike Parker.

All rights reserved. No part of this book may be reproduced, stored in a retrieval system, or transmitted in any form or by any means—electronic, mechanical, photocopy, recording or otherwise—without the prior written permission of the publisher. The only exception is brief quotations for review purposes.
Published by WordCrafts Press
Cody, Wyoming 82414
www.wordcrafts.net

Within every man is a culmination of his boyhood. So it was with young Vlad Dracul, House of Drăculești, born into royalty in a three-story stone house around 1431 in Sighișoara, Transylvania, on the forefront of the epic religious battle between Christian Europe and the Islamic Ottoman Empire.

The Turks sought world domination. A one-man wall stood between them and the whole of Christian Europe.

**Vlad the Impaler,**
**House of Drăculești**
**Defender of the Faith.**

This tale is drawn from little known historical documents, kept hidden by powers that have sought for generations to distort the truth, and keep the world in darkness. But the Truth always has—and always shall—set you free. In the words of Jesus Christ,

*If the world hates you, remember that it hated me first.*
*~Saint John 15:18*

# Capitol Unu

### Tokat Castle, Turkey
### in the Year of our Lord, 1442

*For he is the living God and he endures forever; his kingdom will not be destroyed, his dominion will never end.*

*He rescues and he saves; he performs signs and wonders in the heavens and on the earth. He has rescued Daniel from the power of the lions.*

*~Daniel 6:27*

"Come on, Vlad Drăculea."

Thirteen-year-old Ioana Stathopoulos's soft voice, made softer still by her whispers outside his chamber door, roused the young prince of Wallachia from his sleep. He smiled and rubbed his eyes. The pair of young nobles had been inseparable for so long ago that Vlad, almost twelve, could not remember a time before their friendship. She rapped lightly on his door, something the olive-skinned Grecian beauty always did when her father, the ruler of Hungary known as John Hunyadi, came to stay at the palace that housed the royal family of Wallachia—the Draculesti family.

"Hurry, Vlad," Ioana urged from behind the door. A sense of urgency charged her words. "*Licurici* are not going to catch themselves."

He yawned and glanced toward the window. The night, velvety black and cast with a silvery moon sheen, was the perfect night for catching the little nighttime bugs that flitted about the ground and lit the Wallachian hills with their flashing bodies.

"Hurry," Ioana insisted.

Eyes still heavy with sleep, Vlad tried to hurry as instructed, but his body refused to comply. It was as though he was made of stone. *Ioana,* he thought, *wait for me. I am coming.*

Keys jingled from the other side of the door.

"Vlad . . ." Ioana's voice seemed to be further away. "Hurry . . ."

Vlad, in his dreamlike state, was momentarily confused as the heavy wooden door scraped the stone floor so hard and fast that it banged into the wall behind it without warning nor apology.

"Vlad Drăculea," a masculine voice, replacing the sweet one belonging to Ioana, boomed.

Vlad jerked awake, a familiar twist in his chest as he glanced around the dungeon which had become his home. The dream of beautiful Ioana and his home in Wallachia had begun to fade quicker and quicker as the nights wore on. Still, he clung to the sweet memories as though he was clinging to life itself.

Sobs from the boys, most of them younger than his eleven years, tightened around Vlad Drăculea III's thin shoulders like a death shroud. They echoed off the Turkish dungeon's ancient stone walls and dripped down the damp rock like tears down a betrayed cheek before puddling on the chilly ground around the captives confined there. The prisoners, all foreign boys from European nations, were bound by thick chains and situated between soggy mounds of rotted hay and piles of urine-soaked excrement left disgracefully by whatever humiliated prisoner came before him. There, entwined with the stench, the sobs stayed, moaning quietly, but not silenced, never silenced, among the helpless captives.

No matter how quiet the dungeon of Turkey's Tokat Castle was, no matter how deep the hour of darkness that penetrated its walls, the sobs of the young boys imprisoned there were never silent.

Some cried for their mothers or governesses. Some cried for their fathers or older brothers who had promised to protect them—but failed. Others simply cried. And young Vlad knew precisely why the boys, some of them younger still than his brother Radu's seven years, wept into the damp bosom of darkness that filled Tokat Castle's dilapidated dungeon.

He had cried, too, the first time the big Turk with the golden ring in his nose, a muscled, shirtless man called Abdullah, had burst into the dungeon where prisoners—future soldiers in the Ottoman Empire's Janissary Army—were held, and dragged him across the rocky floor toward the arched stone doorways that led into the castle.

And this time was no different.

Only now, Vlad cried on the inside, not on the outside, where the world could see and where his captors could take even more sick pleasure from his misery.

Abdullah stomped across the fetid floor and unlocked Vlad's chains in the dim light. "Come now," he grumbled, mostly to himself, as he began to drag Vlad across the roughhewn floor by one arm.

A few of the Wallachian boys who had also been handed over by Vlad's father as part of Wallachia's yearly tribute to the Ottoman Empire's Janissary Army, knew for themselves what awaited Vlad when he reached the Sultan's chamber and called out to him in their shared native Romanian tongue.

"The Sultan gets to taste all the new boys before they are turned out to the Turkish court," one called. His voice, silenced with a sharp smack issued by Abdullah's vice-like hand, echoed off the stone walls.

"Submit, Prince Vlad," another called through the rumbling of chains. "Submit and enjoy the comforts of the Turkish court. Save yourself from the hell of this dungeon!"

Vlad's captor held fast to his handcuffed arms and continued to yank him roughly from the rocks of the dungeon floor until his body, still not having found its footing, met the smooth stone path that led deceptively into Tokat Castle's entrails.

There, Abdullah let the dungeon door crash shut behind them with a grunt, effectively silencing the moans and laments of his fellow Wallachians of noble birth.

*My countrymen. Well, at our age, country boys.*

Vlad did not fight too hard against the guard, Abdullah, but he did not trail mindlessly along behind him, either, lest Abdullah get the impression that Vlad was giving up so soon his will to fight. Still, incurring the big man's wrath now would only prove painful to Vlad, and he already knew what awaited him once he reached the Sultan's chambers, and he needed all his rage, all of his fight, to resist the abuse. Instead of fighting and wearing himself out against the inevitable, Vlad leaned back against Abdullah's grip, making himself as heavy as possible, and forced the big Turk to work even harder in his quest to pull him down the pathway.

After a few moments, Abdullah stopped and turned to face the feisty, young Prince Drăculea. A peculiar smile tilted his thin lips beneath his pointed moustache. He spoke to Vlad gruffly, in a strange language that featured a smattering of Turkish punctuated with broken Romanian. "Resist the Sultan's advances, Prince Drăculea, and you will find your quarters to remain in the dungeon. Chained among the rats. Among the thieves. Condemned to *olum*, to death."

†††

"Radu," Vlad called into the dungeon's darkness. "Little brother? *Frate*, are you here?"

"*Dar*," Radu's young voice affirmed. "I am here."

From the darkness, some of the boys cried for their mothers, who no doubt cried for them as well back across the Danube in their home country of Wallachia. Others cried for any relief at all from the pain inflicted upon them by the Turks. A few others, the most morose and desperate who had been imprisoned the longest, cried out to God himself, begging for their Creator to take their souls from their broken, violated bodies before their torturers could return.

Vlad swallowed the lump that had appeared in his throat and tuned out the choir of sobbing Wallachian boys. "Did you resist, Radu?"

His younger brother sighed in the darkness. "*Dar*. But it is getting harder to fight them. They are deliberately feeding us less, are they not?"

"You are correct." Vlad tried to keep his voice steady even though his blood simmered deep within him, entrenched in that hidden place that nobody could reach no matter how deeply they hurt him. "They are using a political strategy against us, *frate*. One that Father and Brother spoke of back in *our* kingdom."

"They did?" Radu sniffed. "I do not remember such things."

"Yes." Vlad cleared his throat and tried not to let his rage, or his fear, shade his words. No good could come from letting Radu sense that he was scared. *Be brave, Vlad. For both of the imprisoned Drăculești princes.* "A hungry enemy," he explained, "is less likely to fight."

Radu's voice, still filled with so much innocence, was muted in the dank darkness. Vlad strained to see his outline, but the overwhelming darkness did not permit it. "Why did Father trade us to these animals?"

*How honest should I be?*

Though some might think him too young to know anything about political warfare, Vlad had been raised every moment of his eleven years at the knee of his father, Vlad Drăculea II, Voivode of Wallachia. He had hidden under his massive desk as men's lives were bartered, condemned, imprisoned, or executed with the stroke of his father's quill pen. Young Vlad remembered well when he first heard of the relatively new practice of the Turks building a janissary army, which proved to be a Turkish army comprised of enslaved Eastern European boys.

However, when the Ottoman Empire's gentle, almost friendly requests for prepubescent boys, to be raised as janissary soldiers loyal to the Turkish cause, transformed into demands for an annual tribute of no less than five hundred Wallachian boys, Vlad shared his worries with his father.

"That will never be you, Mircea, or Radu, so you must not trouble your mind with worries for them," Vlad II had placated him when he asked about the plight of the enslaved boys. "While yes, noble blood courses through their young veins, the Ottomans will never dare enslave any from our royal line."

*Should I tell Radu that our father is a black liar? Well, not completely a liar. He ensured that our older brother, Mircea, was protected from the Ottomans.*

"We are royalty, Radu," Vlad began. "And Father, as ruler of Wallachia, has always been tasked with hard decisions that he alone must make, even if it makes no sense to anyone else. And these do not affect only us as his family, but they are always for the betterment of his entire realm."

"The whole of Wallachia," Radu agreed, "and the whole of the Catholic Church."

"Yes, the whole of Wallachia." Vlad shifted his weight on the unforgiving ground but managed a semblance of a smile. "And yes, for the whole of the Catholic Church."

A calm quiet enveloped the pair of them. "Never forget, *frate*, since Father is a member of the Order of the Dragon, we are, as well."

"A defender of the faith," Radu murmured absently, as though he was reciting a nursery rhyme. "One who protects, fights, and dies for Christendom against any of Her sworn enemies."

"And the halting of the Ottoman advancement into Christian Europe," Vlad finished. Something within his chest swelled with familial pride. "It makes my heart glad that you have remembered."

Vlad wished he could hold his younger brother, like he did when they were back home in Wallachia. However here, there were no rocking chairs in which to rock him. No silken blankets in which

to wrap up against the night's chill. No comforts at all, for neither them nor any of their dungeon mates. "As promised, the Ottomans were marched into Transylvania, in hopes of taking it away from John Hunyadi—"

"Uncle John," Radu mused. "*Athleta Christi*."

"Your Latin is impeccable. You are right, Christ's Champion," Vlad chuckled. "I suppose you could call Hunyadi *uncle*, since he is from Wallachia—"

He tried not to call to mind John Hunyadi too often, because, without fail, when Hunyadi came to his mind, so also came the image of Ioana Stathopoulos.

Radu's voice met his ears again but sounded much further away. "Remember going to spend time at Uncle John's castle in Transylvania? With all the secret passages . . ."

Vlad was powerless to reminisce with his little brother. The recent dream, coupled with the memory of beautiful Ioana had taken control. Only just his senior, the ebony haired Ioana got to call Hunyadi, *father*, but since her mother was not Hunyadi's wife, and was in fact a Greek maid who served the Transylvanian Voivoda, Ioana was never permitted to address him in public at all, and certainly never call him *father*, at least not where others could hear.

Vlad had paid no mind to his own father when he, during one of their many visits to Hunyadi's Transylvanian castle, branded the dusky-hued girl nothing but a worthless bastard of unusual beauty who was destined to either work in a brothel—or own one. Vlad, however, knew she was not worthless, and was destined for greater things than work in a brothel.

During that same visit, Hunyadi took a sunrise leave from the castle to hunt. He ensured Vlad came along, sans his father, who was sleeping off the night's ale in the company of a courtesan, but he also ensured Ioana stole along, as well. Secretly thrilled that the Grecian beauty was in his company, he was astounded by her raw, outdoorsy skill. Not only could Ioana outride him, even on the hilly, Transylvanian terrain, but her archery was impeccable. And the way her sable plaits sailed over her shoulders as she rode—

Radu's voice interrupted his daydream. "Then Hunyadi is family. Is that not what you always say, Vlad? All people of Wallachian ancestry are family?"

Vlad did not answer. Instead, he tried to still his racing heart, which always thumped faster when Ioana came to his mind, and push away the ache in his soul that came with the sweet memories of his carefree childhood.

"Vlad?" Radu tried again. "What about Father?"

Vlad coughed as the image of his Grecian love faded from his mind. "Well, our father promised peace between Wallachia and the Ottoman Empire, because as you might remember, our father fears war more than anything else, even more than the damning of his own soul."

"Vlad, do not say such things. You know hell scares me."

"I am sorry, *frate*." Vlad took care to cool his tongue. "I should not have said that."

Radu's voice was quiet. "Then what happened? With the Ottomans marching into Transylvania?"

"Father promised peace to the Ottomans, but, as a Defender of the Faith, he was also a natural ally of John Hunyadi, the Militant Saint. When time came to choose, the Ottomans were already breaching the Danube, and Father chose to side with Hunyadi, even though he had promised to side with the Ottomans."

Radu's silence spoke volumes. Finally, he dared to speak. "Why did Father promise to be on both sides?"

Vlad spoke quickly. "Because Father does not like conflict. So he goes along, keeping things as peaceful as possible, promising what he will, saying what he must, to ensure that peace lasts as long as possible. However, he forgets what he promised and does not follow what he said, and when the time comes to choose . . ." He let his words hang there.

Radu contemplated this for a moment.

"Is that why the Ottomans lost to Transylvania in that battle?"

Vlad nodded, even though he knew Radu could not see him in the inky darkness of the dungeon. "Yes. And that is why the freshly beaten Ottomans called Father for a meeting in Gallipoli. He was tasked with proving his loyalty to the Ottoman cause. And—" Vlad briefly thought if it was wise to continue and share with his little brother the information he knew but should not have known.

"And?"

Vlad sat in silence.

"*And*, Vlad?"

The elder of the two princes sighed. "And he was told to bring us with him to Gallipoli. Or else."

Radu sat quietly. "And he did as he was told?"

"Obviously."

Radu pieced the rest of the happenings together with no help from Vlad, his innocent voice heavy with truth. "And that is why Father was taken prisoner by the Ottomans the moment we arrived. And why we were also captured and taken away from him. Then brought here, to Tokat Castle. And put in this stinky dungeon."

The words hung there in the humid night air, like a noose.

"You are wise beyond your years, Radu."

The youngest of the Drăculeşti dynasty did not answer. Only quiet sniffles and sobs punctuated the silent dark.

After what seemed an eternal silence, Radu sniffled back the rest of his tears. "I miss Wallachia. I want to go home."

*Wallachia*. Emotion clogged Vlad's throat without warning. *Home*.

Beautiful Wallachia, where the lush grasses spread over the hills that rolled gently away from the castle, like waves on the sea, rolling all the way to the forest's tree line, like an exotic green carpet; thick, expensive, and precious.

Beautiful Wallachia, where he was an intrepid explorer deep within the evergreens that made up the royal forest. Each day, he discovered a thousand new worlds before stopping to nap upon the fallen pine needles in one of his many secret hiding places.

Beautiful Wallachia, with wide blue skies that kissed the tips of the slate gray Transylvanic Alps. Even in the summertime, those distant mountains he swore to summit one day were streaked with snowy fingers of white.

Beautiful Wallachia, where sweet childhood memories lurked like mischievous playmates around every corner in Târgovişte Castle, whose jutting spires and tolling copper chapel bells never neglected to show him the way home, no matter how far he wandered into his beloved woods.

Vlad sucked in a breath and held it. It tasted not of the sweet smells that thickly permeated the Wallachian woods, but instead of rat feces and stale urine—normal for this Turkish dungeon.

Radu was sensitive and soft, like their mother, while he himself took after their hard-browed father. Slowly, he let out the wretched breath he held and tried to ignore the fact that the Wallachia that held all his childhood memories were those of a Wallachia that young Radu would never know.

His baby brother would never stand barefoot on top of the hill by the well, the steepest one in the castle clearing, and fling himself from the top, counting how many times he could roll before reaching the bottom.

*Seven. Seven full rolls from the top of the hill to the bottom. Something Radu will never experience, never know for himself.*

No. Radu's childhood memories would be of this hellish captivity, locked up like an animal by Ottoman hands in an underworld of unspeakable horrors.

Vlad chewed his lip bitterly. *The Ottomans may have put us here, but it was our own father who turned the key to seal our fate.*

"I thought I knew fear, back in Wallachia," Radu sniffed. "Remember? The thunderstorms."

Vlad nodded into the darkness again. During the late autumn nights back home, thunderstorms, born in the mountains, rolled through his beloved forests before crashing into their castle in Târgovişte with all the rage and fury they could muster. When the

whipping wind and pelting rain threatened to burst every window and shatter every stone, Radu would climb into his big brother's lap. Together, they would ignore the eyes that seemed to stare through them from the paintings that lined their nursery walls and rock in their antique rocking chair. Vlad remembered how he would hold Radu close as he whimpered and tell him stories of the brave soldier he would become someday.

"After your fifth birthday, you will brave storms such as these, like all the rest of the Wallachian soldiers. Sometimes, the storms will be even worse, with spinning, black winds and balls of ice pelting you from Heaven itself, yet you will still not be scared."

Radu curled into his chest. "You mean, someday, I will? Go outside in these storms?"

"*Dar*, you will. You will walk into the storm, fearless. Someday, the storm will fear you."

"I cannot be alone."

"You will not be alone. You will be with me and the other Wallachian boys. You will be training to be a fearless warrior for God, come wind or come rain. You do want to be a warrior, do you not?"

Radu's voice grew shrill with fear. "What if I do not want to be a warrior?"

"You will be a great warrior because you were born to be a great warrior," Vlad always continued. "You will be among the toughest of all the boys because you are a Drăculești." He would rock the chair harder as his baby brother clung to him. "You face the storm once, then the next time it will not be so scary. The time after, it will not be scary at all. Then, one day, you will find yourself charging into the storm to face it, head on."

"Like you?"

Vlad nodded and stroked his baby brother's hair. "Like me."

"I am not as brave as you. I never will be."

Vlad rocked the chair, slow and steady, and adjusted the quilt around Radu. "Your time will come, Radu. You will see."

"Vlad?"

"Yes?"

"I am not like those other boys any more than I am like you. What if my time comes and I am still scared?"

Vlad's heart broke for little, tender Radu. "Then I will protect you. I will always protect you."

"Promise?"

"On the honor of the Drăculeşti dynasty, I promise."

After many whispered assurances to the youngest of the Drăculeşti brothers that, no matter what horrors the thunderstorms brought to the family castle, Vlad would let no harm come to him and that he would always be there to protect him, Radu would drift off to an uneasy sleep.

*Please God*, Vlad would pray after Radu's beathing had become the deep, rhythmic breathing of sleep. *Please do not let me make empty promises that I cannot keep—like our father.*

Vlad shook off the memories of the thunderstorms and closed his eyes against the darkness of the dungeon. When one memory of Wallachia came to his mind, no matter how hard he tried to stem them, more memories followed. After only a moment, the memories were washing over him like a swollen river.

*Please God, let Radu hold on to what few memories of Wallachia he has.*

Despite his prayer, he was powerless to disremember the flood of memories that threatened to drown him.

# Capitol Doi

### Tokat Castle, Turkey
### in the Year of our Lord, 1442

*Remember that at that time you were separate from Christ, excluded from citizenship in Israel and foreigners to the covenants of the promise, without hope and without God in the world.*

*~Ephesians 2:12*

Vlad kept his eyes closed tightly as the surge of memories swelled and loomed. The face of his older brother, Mircea, filled his mind. He had never bothered to assure Vlad of unending protection when it was just the two of them in the years before Radu was born. Mircea was much too busy training, and, as the rightful heir to the throne of the Wallachian kingdom, he was tasked with following their father, Vlad II, every waking moment. Despite his youth, Vlad understood the reasons, but he still wished Mircea were to him what he hoped he was to Radu.

As for their illegitimate older brother, Vlad the Monk? He was never around at all, nor was he permitted to be spoken of, on pain of severe punishment. It was as if their eldest brother had, at their shared father's whim, simply ceased to exist.

Vlad forced open his eyes and sighed into the dark. "If Father was a regular Wallachian nobody, he never would have brought us here." He knew this was a tricky subject and hard to explain, especially to a child. He was not even entirely certain that he understood it completely himself. At least not in his heart. "But we are not Wallachian nobodies, Radu. We are royalty, the heirs to the throne of Wallachia, the future of the House of Drăculeşti."

As if on some divine cue, the clouds rolled back and revealed the silvery moon through the high, rough-cut windows of the Turkish prison. Radu was no more than an arm's length away.

Their eyes, squinty from the sudden brightness, met, and Radu's hand breached the small expanse and caught Vlad's. He sniffled, and his dark eyes filled with moisture.

Vlad's words came faster. "Our family is a political one, *frate*. Father must maintain foreign relations, and part of that is making deals."

"I wish he had not brought us with him."

The memories soured in Vlad's mind.

*I wish I could protect you from the storm that is our father.*

It was rare that Vlad let thoughts of their father pollute his mind. Thinking of his father made him angry, and it did not do to get angry while locked in a dungeon. Still, he let the memories come, along with the anger that came with them.

"We will be south of the Danube for only a short while," a smiling Vlad II had assured his two youngest sons on the road from Târgovişte, Wallachia, to Gallipoli in the Ottoman Empire. "As princes of Wallachia, you must see how diplomacy is maintained between very different countries."

Mentally, Vlad caught his father in that lie. *He was ordered to bring us*, he wanted to shout. *This is not an educational exercise.* However, young Vlad held his tongue and said nothing.

The moment they crossed the Danube, Ottoman forces, which had been waiting in the shadows, emerged.

"We are here to escort you to Gallipoli," one large Turk, who looked much like Abdullah, explained.

In that fleeting moment, Vlad caught a flicker of fear across his father's eyes.

"Nay, we are fully capable of making the trip ourselves. We have come this far, have we not?"

Several Ottoman soldiers moved to encircle them as the leader shook his head and smiled. His voice was sickeningly soft and sweet. "You traveled across your own country. Now, you are in a hostile country. You assured, when you sided with Hungary, that we are now enemies, did you not?"

His father was silent.

"So," the Turk continued as he took hold of the Voivode of Wallachia's reins, "allow us to do you the *honor* of escorting you across this hostile land. For the sake of ensuring your safety and the safety of your young heirs, of course."

"I—" The elder Vlad began.

The large Turk cut him off and barked an order at the Ottoman soldiers that had flanked Vlad and Radu. "Do take the boys to Tokat Castle, where lodgings have been aptly prepared for them."

Vlad's father attempted to speak again but was silenced.

"And you sir?" the captor continued. "You shall accompany me to Gallipoli where the Sultan anxiously awaits a word with you."

Vlad II cast a look over his shoulder to his sons. Young Vlad could not rightly understand the look, but deep in his bones, he knew he would never see his father again.

Radu's voice interrupted his sour reverie.

"Do you think Father is still in prison in Gallipoli, Vlad?"

Vlad rubbed the bridge of his nose and glanced at Radu.

Eyes wide with concern for the man who stole their childhoods and gave them willingly into the hands of the enemy, Radu's loving innocence pricked at Vlad's heart in places he thought it was much too hard to be pricked.

*Honest. Be honest. If he is old enough to ask, he is deserving of an honest answer.* "The Ottomans, they showed me letters. I cannot be certain they were authentic. They told of what happened to Father."

Radu's hands, hands that used to be so chubby and warm but were now thin and cold, gripped his fingers. "What did they say?"

"The letters said that it did not take long for Vlad II, Voivode of Wallachia, to weasel out of Ottoman captivity. After all, his safety back to Wallachia, and to his throne, was guaranteed—if he agreed to leave you and me in Ottoman care. Which he did."

Vlad bit his tongue to keep from telling the rest. *And furthermore, he agreed to peace with these barbarians on pain of* our *deaths, Radu's and mine. While his life was given back to him with pomp and glory.*

The tell-tale red ring, the one that came with thoughts of their father and anything else that incited anger within him, colored Vlad's vision.

"Do you think the letters was authentic?" Radu's small voice rolled over the big word that he had never used until now.

"*Dar.*" Vlad whispered. "I do."

"I do not like it here." Radu's voice, suddenly threatening hysteria, made Vlad jump. "I want to go home, Vlad. I want to go home now. To Mother."

Vlad tried to ignore the helpless twang in his brother's words and the pull it had in his chest. "We are princes, Radu. We must be strong and represent Wallachia well. In doing this, we will make Father and Mother proud." He squeezed Radu's hand, even though his was shaking. "We will not be held in captivity long. Father will send for us once peace with the Ottomans is secure. Have faith, *frate.*"

Radu hung his head. A tear dripped from his eye as the inky clouds covered the moon and left them cloaked in total darkness once again.

"We can live with the pain, for we know it is a gift from our captors and only ours for a short while. We are warrior princes, made for such tough trials as these." The brio of Vlad's voice gave even himself a newfound sense of Wallachian pride. "But the shame of giving into their black lusts and demonic demands, we could never live with that."

Radu sniffled in the darkness again. Vlad knew he was crying.

"Here, pray with me now. In Latin." Vlad did the sign of the cross. "*In nomine Patris, et Filii, et Spiritus Sancti.*"

Radu's hand slipped from his as he imitated Vlad and mumbled the ancient words.

At what seemed like an odd place on the wall, one of the many doors that led into the dungeon flew open. Candlelight flooded into the freshly fallen darkness and chased away the shadows. Giant rats skittered this way and that as they squeaked angrily at the light's intrusion into their dark, fetid world.

"Radu Drăculea," a booming voice called, almost mockingly. "Come Prince Drăculeşti, it is time for your lessons."

"*Ave Maria, gratia plena,*" Vlad whispered. "Be strong, Radu. Be strong. No shame."

The man with the booming voice strode with commanding steps across the chilly rock floor.

"*Dominus tecum.*"

"Where are they taking me, Vlad?" Radu sounded like a terrified child. Which he was.

"To your tutor." Vlad grabbed Radu's hand as it searched fervently for his. "Remember, you and I are royalty. We are *guests* here. Not prisoners."

*It is the storm all over again. And I cannot protect him.*

The words soured on his tongue and fell into his gut like cold stones as the big man yanked Radu from his grasp.

"Come, *Prince*."

Radu whimpered as the man pulled him to his feet.

Lying went against everything Vlad believed in, but it was apparent that Radu was struggling to keep a tight hold on their faith—a faith which was certainly being tested now.

Their father's face filled Vlad's mind again as the man led Radu across the dungeon. He jumped as the door slammed behind his little *frate*, a boy who trailed helpless innocence like a vulture trailed the sick and dying.

Vlad II, Voivode of Wallachia, had dealt them into the hands of the devil to secure a peaceful reign for himself and the oldest of the legitimate Drăculeşti brothers, Mircea, who would succeed him. His father was always a careful strategist, normally to the benefit of the whole of the Drăculeşti family.

*Not this time, Father. You have failed Radu and me.*

The rest of the prayer flew off Vlad's lips as he stared at the closed dungeon door that blended so expertly into the dungeon wall. "*Benedicta tu in mulieribus, et benedictus fructus ventris tui, Iesus. Sancta Maria, Mater Dei, ora pro nobis peccatoribus, nunc et in hora mortis nostrae. Amen.*"

Vlad sucked in a deep breath. Under normal circumstances—or what had become normal since coming to Turkey—praying a Hail Mary made him feel better.

Not tonight.

Tonight, he could only think of helpless Radu, the young boy whose fear had almost been tangible as they prayed together before the big man took him away. Radu's fear, thick like a winter blanket, still hung about Vlad like a heavy cloak. His prayer tonight was a call to arms.

He balled his fists at his side. The chains that made heavy his arms rattled as he moved. He studied them closer. While it was true, he was draped in chains, Vlad was pleasantly surprised to learn that they were not locked around his wrists.

His heartbeat quickened to a gallop in his chest, and words passed his lips in a whisper. "The guards, drunken fools that they are, neglected to lock me back into my shackles after they returned me from the Sultan's chambers."

*Father is a careful strategist. And I can be, too.*

Slowly, Vlad eased himself from the cold floor and inched toward where he thought the door had been. A rat screeched as he stepped on it. Heart thundering in his chest, he wished for a dagger or even a stick. Alas, he found himself with no weapon with which to defend himself. Still, if the Turks were lying about taking Radu

to tutoring, as they were known to do, Vlad was not sure his little brother was strong enough to resist any longer.

*Only I will not forget our family, Father. My strategy will be for the betterment of both your forgotten sons.*

"Prince Vlad," someone whispered from the darkness. "Pray for me. My body aches so."

The moon showed herself from behind her veil of clouds. He glanced over his shoulder. A Wallachian boy, his age and bathed in moonlight, lifted his head from the floor. He looked tall, perhaps even taller than him. His pale lips pulled up into some semblance of a smile as his tired eyes met those of his prince. "Please, I beg you."

Vlad softened his gaze toward his fellow countryman. "What is your name?"

"Luca. My name is Luca Snagov, Your Grace."

Vlad nodded to Luca, loyal subject that he was, and did the Sign of the Cross in his direction. "May God, keep you, Luca Snagov, in His Merciful Hand. Our Father, who art in Heaven, in Your infinite mercy, forget not your Wallachian sons at the hands of the Ottoman devils."

Luca's eyes closed, and a look of peace befell his haggard face. "Thank you, Prince Vlad." He lowered his head back onto a mound of rotting straw.

Vlad nodded as he turned and felt his way along the wall, his thin fingers searching for any crack, any nook that led to any one of the countless camouflaged doors that led into the dungeon. His thumb brushed over an infinitesimal crack along the surface of the wall.

*This door here. This is the one they came through to take Radu.*

Vlad dug his nimble fingers into the crack and worked at it. After a moment, the door, not meant to be opened from the inside, creaked in protest before consenting to open. The same light from before forced its way back into the darkness of the dungeon. He squinted against the sudden brightness and peeked into the ornate hallway.

It was empty.

Quietly, Vlad slipped into the hall, his mind on the end of his Latin prayer.

*Please do pray for me, Mother Mary. For my hour of death may be near.*

# Capitol Trei

Tokat Castle, Turkey
in the Year of our Lord, 1442

*Fear thou not, for I am with thee.*

*~Isaiah 41:10*

Candlelit hallways spread out before him in all directions like spider's legs, crooked and nonsensical. With his back pressed against the cobblestone wall, Vlad crept down the hallway. Voices that chattered in Arabic wafted from out of the numerous rooms and seemed to surround him. He narrowed his eyes and slowed his breathing from what was rapid puffs to slow, deep breaths. Despite the chattering that continued, Vlad thankfully saw nobody.

*Radu, where are you?*

Vlad crept along, his back against the wall, until another hallway cut in front of him. He stopped.

*Right here, I am out in the open.* If anyone comes from any direction— His heart threatened to pound out of his chest. *I will be caught. And if I get caught—*

A rogue memory flashed into his young mind. Mircea had come into the nursery where he and Radu, who was just beginning to toddle, were waiting for their governess to arrive. She was to escort them to the morning meal, and the noises from Vlad's stomach told of her tardiness.

"Go watch from the window," Mircea instructed.

Vlad gripped his stomach and tried not to act hungry. "What am I watching for?"

Mircea's lips, full like their mother's, pulled up into the sort of mischievous grin that only an older brother can make. "You will know when you see. Now go to the window and wait."

Before the door fell shut behind his oldest brother, Vlad plastered himself against the nursery window, as instructed. A mob had grown outside the castle gate. Some of the people yelled and pumped their fists into the air, while others, mostly women, hung their heads and sobbed loudly. From somewhere that Vlad could not see, someone blew a trumpet, and the castle gates opened. Obediently, the thrumming crowd shushed.

A few moments later, Mircea and their father, the Voivode, emerged, flanked by soldiers perched smartly atop decorated horses. The freshly shushed crowed parted before them, as the Red Sea had parted before Moses in the days of old. Both Mircea and their father held a rope and, behind their war horses, led two broken, bloodied, naked men.

Vlad had been trying feverishly to get Radu to quit wiggling and watch with him, but at the sight of the naked men, he put his little brother back down. In his mind's eye, Vlad recognized the men as Turks.

A few broken words, words that held no meaning to him as a child, met his ears. "*Visitors in our land*," and "*homosexual practices*," and "*punishable by death*," and "*against natural law*," came together to create a feeling of doom for the two men as they were led by his beloved father and brother from the castle and through the crowd. There, before them on the horizon, newly-knotted ropes swung from the gallows.

Waiting.

Hungry.

The men were led, like sheep, up the gallows steps. The hangman, a hooded man who appeared seemingly from nowhere, placed the heads of the naked prisoners into the nooses. The mob followed them the short distance and stood nearby. Women began to wail afresh, and Vlad felt the energy from the entire scene as it drew to a climax. Radu, finally interested, stood on his tiptoes, and babbled as he smacked the window with one pudgy hand.

Outside, Mircea spoke a few words that Vlad could not hear, made a motion with his arm, then—*Crack*.

The executions of the two half-dead Turkish men were carried out quickly and without much fanfare.

The two men, moments ago walking and bleeding, swung there, dead, like broken limbs from an old tree. Nobody moved to collect the bodies, so freshly devoid of life—not even the women who had shed so many wailing tears over them.

The mob melted into the landscape as Mircea and Father rode back to the castle on prancing horses. No emotion registered on their faces as they passed beneath Vlad's nursery window until Mircea looked up and waved.

Something in Vlad's empty stomach turned over when he saw that Mircea, his beloved brother, was grinning.

"Stop, you!" The sound of Radu's young, excited voice shook him from his daydream. "I said do not touch me!"

A platter clattered to the floor as a bunch of fat, purple grapes rolled into the hallway.

*I found you, Little Brother.*

Radu, however, did not realize that he had been found. Like a bolt of lightning from a low hanging cloud, Radu jumped over the platter of grapes and bounded down the hallway like a hare . . . and the bloodhounds were not far behind.

Men chattered in Arabic, loud and fast, and dashed out of the room, with their white robes billowing behind them.

Vlad dared not draw a breath as he pressed his back against the wall and closed his eyes as the clamoring of the men grew louder.

And nearer.

And nearer still.

With their robes whooshing behind them, the men passed him, intent only on catching his innocent baby brother. Without an inkling of a thought for his own safety, Vlad fell in behind them.

They continued down the hall until the light from the candelabras that festooned the walls dimmed further and further, until they were running in absolute darkness, the same kind of damp darkness that was present in his dungeon. Before Vlad could think about where they had gotten to, the darkness gave way to something else.

Fresh air.

*We are outside.* The realization of his predicament was as terrifying as it was thrilling.

The increasingly real possibility of being discovered urged him backward until his back was plastered against the cold facade of Tokat Castle. As his eyes adjusted in the cool of the dark, Vlad glanced around. *We are in a courtyard of some sort, a courtyard that surrounds the castle.*

Taking care to be silent, Vlad glanced to his right and studied the opening from whence they had emerged. *This is not a typical castle. This is a secret entrance through the mouth of a small cave.*

From out of the darkness, the voices of the men he had followed met his ears. They had split up, or so it sounded, and were laughing and poking fun at each other. It was as though chasing his terrified *frate* through the castle and into the darkness was nothing more than a game to them. Vlad squatted lower against the wall as the realization of what was happening lit a burning anger within him.

*How dare they laugh at the heirs to the Wallachian throne? How dare they laugh at the children of God in with their heathen cackles, as though my brother's fear is there only for their amusement?*

Vlad's blood began to simmer.

Without warning, the moon once again showed herself from behind her veil of clouds and forced Vlad to duck lower still behind a scrubby thorn bush.

*"Psst."*

The men crept about the courtyard like leashed wildcats on the scent of prey, intent on finding his baby brother. Vlad glanced about, but even in the moonlight; he could see no hint of Radu anywhere.

*"Psst!"*

Vlad looked up above him. There, ensnared in the branches of the scrubby thorn bush which concealed him, was Radu. Bloody and tangled, but as of yet, undiscovered. Vlad released the breath he did not realize that he had been holding.

"Aha!" Someone grabbed Vlad's shoulders. "Got you!"

*If they have me, perhaps they will tire of looking for Radu.*

For the first time since arriving at Tokat Castle, Vlad allowed himself to be dragged inside without a fight.

The boisterous laughter of the men, so proud in claiming their obvious prize, hung in his ears as they dragged him through the halls.

"Hey, is this the same boy?" The man who had clamped his hands onto Vlad's shoulders gave him a little shake. "I think this boy is heavier."

His comrade spoke through his laughter. "Why would *two* boys be in the courtyard?"

Vlad clamped his mouth shut and resisted the urge to yell at his captors, as he normally did.

"Ahmed bey, you have been smoking too much. You cannot even tell one boy from the other."

Vlad's captor stopped walking and bent down until they were eye level. "The next time you pull a stunt like that, you will get ten stripes with—"

Vlad stared back, like he had seen cornered vipers do. Unflinching. Unblinking. Unmoving.

"Hey," his captor's voice changed from scolding to scathing, "I know you."

The other man stepped to his side and grasped Vlad's other arm. He was no longer laughing.

Vlad felt his lips pull back in a black grimace, but he did not care. Somewhere in his mind, he prayed that Radu had enough time to untangle himself from the thorns and climb out of the tree. *Be on your way home, Little Brother, running full speed back to Wallachia.*

"This is the boy's brother," he chided. "The *older* of the two princes."

His mocking tone soured in Vlad's ears. Without thinking too far into the future of the repercussions that were certain to follow, Vlad pooled a mouthful of spittle on his tongue and spat it full force into Ahmed's face. The lanky captor with the angry face, now wet with spittle, stumbled back in surprise.

"Why you little—" Ahmed did not bother to finish his insult. Instead, he pulled back his arm and smacked Vlad hard across the face. So hard the eleven-year-old crashed into the wall with a bone-jarring thud.

The nameless of the two men plucked him up at once. "Seems someone forgot to shackle you, *Prince*."

Ahmed wiped the spit from his face and stared at Vlad with stormy eyes.

"A prince is an heir to the throne of a kingdom," Ahmed seethed. "These Wallachian boys were turned out by their father, just to keep peace in his realm. Their cowardly father is a worm, and these two are runts of the litter. No more heir to anything than a *dog*."

A tell-tale red ring tinted Vlad's vision as the men's hands held him tighter, like iron.

"Tie him in the study," Ahmed growled. "I have grown tired of his games. Now, we shall exact from him what we want—what is our *right*. And teach him what submission truly means."

Vlad's voice rolled out of his throat like a cornered dog in a mismatched fight to the death. "You will burn in hell for eternity. Both of you."

"Hell?" Both men exchanged bemused glances. "Stupid non-believer. A harem of virgins awaits us in the afterlife."

Their laughter echoed in the halls as they dragged Vlad, now

kicking and fighting with all of his might, down the stone pathway to the study.

Vlad was mostly unconscious when Ahmed tossed him back into his dungeon prison, his body bloody and broken. He lay there, unmoving and barely breathing, until the gnawing of the rats on his exposed skin forced him fully awake. Vlad kicked them off and, at once, regretted moving. He groaned.

"Prince, thank God you are alive," came a voice from the darkness.

"We thought they succeeded in killing you," another agreed.

Vlad tried to sit up, but the world spun around him. He lay back in the rotted straw that the rats had claimed as their own. Jaw swollen almost shut, he could only manage one word, the only word that mattered. "Radu?"

"They brought him in some time after they brought you, Prince." The voice paused. "He has not yet awakened."

Vlad forced himself to sit up, despite the stabbing pains that came from everywhere and the pitching and swirling of everything in his vision. Whatever they had done to him, it had almost broken him. *In body*, Vlad corrected his thought. *But not in spirit*.

Blinded by darkness, he began to pat the ground around him, as much as the heavy, too-tight iron shackles that bit into his wrists would allow. *Seems they are making up for not having shackled me before.*

"Radu? *Unde eşti? Frate*, where are you, little brother?" His chains rattled hopelessly as he was shackled by the wrists, the ankles, and around the middle. "*Unde eşti?*"

The silence was deafening as every Wallachian boy who resisted the Turks—and were forced to occupy the dungeon because of it—waited. Some barely breathed. Vlad sat still as possible, so his chains made no noise.

Someone sucked in a shuddering breath. Then groaned.

A wave of relief threatened to drown Vlad as he recognized the familiar groan in an instant. Tears pooled in his eyes, and his lower lip quivered. "Radu, little brother, praise God. You are alive."

"Am I?" Something moved in the darkness.

"Yes." Vlad tried to smile, despite his hurt and swollen face.

"I wish I was dead, then I would not hurt so."

Before Vlad could answer him, before he could reassure him to fight with every ounce of his strength no matter the pain they inflicted, Radu *hmphed*.

Vlad imagined his little brother pushing himself up in the rotted straw. "I tried to resist, Vlad. But I was not given the opportunity."

Vlad waited a moment, then asked the question he was not certain he wanted to know the answer to. "What happened?"

Radu's young voice was strained. "I hid in the thorn bush after you let them pull you inside." He paused. "I knew you did that on purpose."

"You did?"

"Yes." Radu sounded tired. Too tired. "You have never done anything willingly here."

*Thank you, God, for letting Radu see that in my example.*

"I planned on climbing down. I knew the timing was important." Radu groaned before continuing. "When I did, the courtyard was empty. If the Sultan had not come out to urinate when I was scaling the wall I would have been on my way to Wallachia. I knew you risked your life for me, and I was not going to waste that chance." The heartbroken note in Radu's voice tugged and twisted in Vlad's chest. "I knew you would fight them off and come after me. I did not want you to have to look for me, and risk getting caught again . . ."

"You have the mind of a warrior prince, Radu. That is exactly what I was thinking, too."

Radu sighed, but something hitched in his throat making it sound jagged. "But he grabbed me and yanked me off the wall. I could not escape."

"Sultan Murad II himself did so?"

"*Dar*. He grabbed me. And I knew I could not escape, but I remembered what you said about fighting until the last breath."

Vlad's eyebrows shot skyward in admiration. "You *fought* the Sultan?"

"I wrestled his dagger from him. I tried to stab him in the neck, but he hit my arm. So I jabbed at his chest, but he knocked me down. All I managed to do was slice his leg."

"Good." Vlad's heart swelled with pride for his little brother. "You did very, very good, Radu."

"I hoped I was doing good. I did not want to get dragged back inside, because I knew what they wanted to do to me. But then, more men came. They took my dagger, then dragged me inside anyway." His voice cracked. "And did unspeakable things, Vlad, in unspeakable ways. They hurt me over and over. And they laughed while they did so, even though I cried and cried and begged them to stop." Another hitch in his voice broke his story. "I thought they were going to kill me, Vlad." His hopeless words hung in the dungeon atmosphere for all the Wallachian boys to hear. "I wish they had."

The aches and stabbing pains in Vlad's body fizzled away as the burning hatred for the Turks boiled to life within him. His shackles clinked as his tingling hands balled into fists.

"Can you forgive me for not being successful in resisting better?" Radu's voice was damp was sobs. "Can God forgive me?"

"There is nothing to forgive, Radu. You have not sinned. However, you have been sinned against. Grievously."

A door, always a different door than the one before, flung open. Light flooded into the dark dungeon. Vlad shushed and squinted his eyes.

"The tutor has arrived and is prepared to school each of you heathen Wallachian non-believers." Vlad recognized the man's voice from the night before.

*Ahmed.*

"Today," the Ottoman prince continued, "I will take you all at once." He paused and stared blackly at Vlad. "And may Allah be with you if you choose to disobey and make a mockery of my leniency."

## Capitol Patru

Târgovişte Castle, Wallachia
in the Year of our Lord, 1442

*For it is not an enemy who taunts me, then I could bear it;*
*It is not an adversary who deals insolently with me, then I could hide from him.*
*But it is you, a man, my equal, my companion, my familiar friend.*

*~Psalm 55:12–15*

Dearest Sultan Murad II,
Supreme Ruler of the Ottoman Empire:
I humbly thank you for hosting me in your country by way of Gallipoli and ensuring my safe return to my kingdom. Again, my deepest apologies for Transylvanian leader John Hunyadi's routing of Ottoman forces in Wallachia. Those precious lives, forever broken by my untrustworthy ally, will never be replaced nor will they be forgotten. Rest assured that Ottoman blood is as welcome in my country as is Wallachian blood, so long as I sit on the throne.

I am forever indebted to you and your men for my quiet return to my rightful throne that you, in your unending wisdom and kindness, saw fit that I keep.

As per our agreement, I have dispatched riders to bring you no less

DEFENDER OF THE FAITH

*than 500 Wallachian boys, most of noble birth, to join the ranks of my youngest sons, Vlad III and Radu. I heartily entreat them to your loving care, and I trust that they shall serve as worthy tributes in your Janissary army.*

*Along with the young future soldiers, find enclosed my first payment of 10,000 gold coins, which will be paid to the Ottoman Empire annually from my country of Wallachia, so long as the Drăculești line occupies the throne. In turn, the Ottomans will find an eternal friend in Wallachia, which will render any need to cross the Danube in a hostile manner unnecessary on either of our countries's parts.*

*Your ever-humble ally and friend,*
*Vlad II, House of Drăculești, Voivode of Wallachia*

†††

Mircea shifted his weight as he stood, alone with his father, in the Targoviste Castle writing room. Brightly painted frescoes adorned the deep, wooden walls that depicted generations of Saints with their bright, golden halos, and were pockmarked with the stern-faced Wallachian leaders of yesteryear. The scent of pine pitch and cedar hung heavy in the air, a scent that Mircea used to find incredibly comforting. The warm crackling of the fire that roared from the fireplace that covered the entirety of the far wall once made this room Mircea's favorite. Today though, it did not have the same effect.

Vlad II's giant mahogany desk, one that he had inherited from his father and that his father had inherited from his father before him, dominated the writing room and was piled high with papers, edicts, and scrolls. In the midst of the mess, the Moldavian wax, purple in color, that would seal the letter to the Turkish devil Murad II himself, melted in a bronze cauldron over a candle flame.

Mircea licked his lips and tried not to fidget. It was never a healthy practice to criticize or question a ruler, especially not a ruler whose mind you did not trust. And Mircea did not trust the mind of Voivode Vlad Drăculea II, even though that same ruler was his father.

"How did you find the Sultan?" The words were off Mircea's tongue with more incredulity than he had intended.

Vlad II gave his eldest legitimate son and heir, a sharp, sideways look.

"Ah, bah," Mircea babbled, "and does he know how grateful and how blessed are we that he allowed you to return home to your rightful throne, Wallachia?"

Vlad II turned his attention from his heir to the monstrous desk. He admired his reflection in a piece of glass rimmed with a golden frame that sat atop the fine desk, nestled between parchment, wells, and quills. With a grunt, he drew his fingers down the length of his moustache and paused at the severe point, turning his head this way and that so that he could admire himself from every angle.

"How did I find the Sultan, you ask? The Sultan was . . ."

A stream of purple wax bubbled over from its brass cauldron and hissed as it sizzled in the candleflame. Without fanfare, Vlad II abandoned his thought in mid-sentence and folded the letter he had penned to the Sultan into thirds. Deep in concentration, he produced a pair of ribbons, red and gold from his messy desk and laid them carefully over the letter's opening. Before Mircea could evoke an answer from his father, Vlad II poured a puddle of wax over the top of the ribbons. Before the wax could harden, he took out his personal seal, a metal stamp complete with thick wooden handle, and thrust it into the pool of bubbly wax.

"How did I find the Sultan, you say?"

Mircea coughed. "Yes."

"I found the Sultan to be a fat old man whose beliefs play trickery with reality. He may be imprudent, but he is *rich*, powerful, and imprudent."

When he pulled his personal stamp from the wax embossment, a fierce, forked-tongued dragon curled about where moments before only the bubbly wax had been.

Mircea exhaled.

Vlad II held the letter out to his son. "We are of a great family dynasty, Mircea. The Order of the Dragon. The Sultan respects that. Him keeping me prisoner—" Vlad II shrugged as though he was merely dismissing a dessert that had not tasted as sweet as it should have. "Political fun and games, my boy. All political fun and games. After all, why would a man bother to strengthen his muscles if he did not plan to flex them for the whole of the world to see once in a while?"

Mircea accepted the letter. *If I thrust this envelope with enough force, would it impale itself upon Father's severe moustache?* He shook his head. "And where does that leave the Drăculeşti family, Father? Does it leave us in a position to flex our muscles as well?"

Vlad II removed the wax melting pot from over the candle and stared into the flame. "Like our namesake, the dragon, we will bide our time. Only when the timing is right will the Drăculeşti dynasty show its power to the world. And it will not be a show of force, but it will truly be a crushing blow upon our enemies."

"Our enemies." Mircea turned the letter over in his hands. "Would our enemies be the Ottomans? Or the Hungarians?"

Vlad II drew his gaze away from the flame and stared hard at his eldest son. "Now you are thinking like a leader."

Mircea shrunk under his father's hard stare and tried not to let his confusion show. "But Father—"

Vlad II's gaze softened. He waved a dismissive hand at his eldest son. "Ensure that letter finds its way into the proper hands."

Mircea hung his head and trudged to the door. He wanted so to freely question his father, as he had when he was younger. He would climb onto his father's lap as he ruled, doled out punishments, and made decisions with his trademark hard-browed authority. Those were the days he could ask anything and expect an honest answer; the days when he knew his father's mind and loved him with his whole heart.

These days, however, love within the castle walls was as foreign to him as were the ways of the Ottomans. Any presumably wrong word was enough to send the elder Wallachian ruler into a murderous rage.

Mircea knew he should not speak again, having already been dismissed. He also knew how his father did not appreciate being questioned about his tactics in governing, war, or politics. Mircea sucked in a sharp breath and glanced over his shoulder.

Vlad II was again staring into the flame of the wax-melting candle, seemingly completely unaware of his son's presence.

"Father?"

"Hmm?"

Mircea cleared his throat. "Are Vlad and Radu . . ." He cleared his throat again. If the Ottomans were truly an ally and not an enemy, as he and the whole of Wallachia previously thought, it would be unwise—and potentially life threatening—to let on that he was suspicious of them.

His brothers' young faces flashed in his mind. The strain that would ripple over Vlad's face when he tried so hard during rainy training days but refused to give up. The wide-eyed innocence that made him feel as though he should protect little Radu at all costs. *I used to sneak sweets into the nursery and hide them in their beds.* A nostalgic ache twisted in his chest. *God Almighty, I wish I had told them it was me who left those treats for them.* Both looked up to him, depended on him, but it was Father who forced him to be strong and absent from his baby brothers for most all of their lives. "Learn to rule," was the Voivode's mantra, which made it a universal truth among the boys. Now, his brothers were gone, under the supposed care of their mortal enemies, and the illustrious, all-knowing, all-powerful leader of Wallachia, who spent his days staring into a candle flame, had not done so much as lifted a finger to bring them home.

*Is it not true that wars are fought over such things? Is it not true that these are the things that God has permitted us to murder—and to die—for?* The ever-present thought swirled in his mind like a fever plague. *Mircea, you fool. How can you think of charging off to war if you cannot even ask your father a simple question?*

He straightened his back and turned to face the Voivode. "How are we to be certain Vlad and Radu are receiving the best possible treatment?" The authoritative tone in his voice caught the both of them off guard.

Slowly, Vlad II rose from his velvet covered chair. Something gleamed in his eyes, and Mircea was not entirely sure he wanted to know what it was. "Do you have reason to believe the Sultan would treat my sons with anything less than the proper respect due to princes?"

Mircea dared not blink. "Father—"

Vlad II struck out with his fist and smacked the wooden door, just shy of Mircea's head. He flinched hard and closed his eyes.

"I am not your father! I am your Voivode!"

Mircea forced a swallow. From somewhere, he willed the courage he wished he had when sneaking the sweets anonymously into his brothers' nursery. He steeled his backbone and stared over his father's shoulder, out the window. "Your Highness," he shouted, as a soldier might answer his commanding officer on the battlefield, "how can we, as Wallachian royalty, ensure the well-being of our princes whilst under the care of persons who are as shifting as the sands in their allegiance to our promises of peace?"

Vlad II's moustache twitched, and his mouth transformed from a scowl into a hard line. "State your meaning."

"The blood of our royal family is too precious to entrust to anyone. Especially not fair-weather friends." Mircea shifted his weight and ignored the knot that formed in his throat. "Or foes."

Vlad II let out a massive roar. His hands flew out and, for an instant, Mircea was certain that he had breathed his last. Instead, his father grabbed him and pulled him close, something he had not done in years. "Mark this day and strike a coin," he yelled to the absent room. "Your future Wallachian Voivode has aligned his mind to that of a ruler!"

Mircea's eyebrows arched skyward, but he did not return his father's embrace.

"Come," Vlad II demanded. "We have executions to perform. Thieves and adulterers await our arrival."

He led his son into the hallway. "Oh," he added absently, "do add five more gold pieces to the purse bound for the Sultan. For care and keeping of the princes."

## Capitol Cinci

Tokat Castle, Turkey
in the Year of our Lord, 1443

*Be alert and of sober mind. Your enemy, the devil, prowls around like a roaring lion looking for someone to devour.*
*~1 Peter 5:8*

Seven Wallachian boys, each dressed in identical, flowing Persian robes, sat around an oval table somewhere deep within in the twining, recessed halls of Tokat Castle. This particular room was called the study, and once upon a time, it was Vlad's favorite room. Books stacked to the ceiling on oddly shaped shelves boasted titles in a multitude of languages, such as French, Spanish, English, Romanian, and Persian. Old and dusty as they were, they still smelled of knowledge, something Vlad once craved.

Their smiling, Latin-speaking tutor, Master Emine, whose tall white turban blocked out most of the window behind him, stood before his misbegotten class of boys, six of whom beamed back at him.

Days when the tutor came were the best days, filled with snacks, rest, talk, learning, and reading. Best of all, on days when the tutor came marked a day they were not in the dungeon. Despite his grinning counterparts, Vlad's face resembled more of a storm cloud.

"Nicolae, Luca, Andrei, Radu, Ștefan, Măriuca. You are coming along quite well in your Aristotelian philosophy, but one among you has set the course to master the subject." The brown-skinned tutor with the the thick, Arabic accent, waved his quill pen in the air. "Prince Vlad, please stand and be recognized by your peers and by your betters."

Vlad liked Master Emine well enough and took care never to be contemptuous or disrespectful to him in any sense. His tutor always treated him with respect, even when his guards—especially Ahmed—insisted he be treated like a mangy dog worthy of no more than kicks or hits.

Once, Vlad overheard a conversation he never should have been privy to. Ahmed's voice was most distinct.

"Master Emine, Vlad Drăculea is to be punished as much as possible. He refuses to submit to our ways, *Allah's* ways, and fights us at every turn."

"Yes, report to us even the smallest infraction, so the boy might be punished accordingly. Cat o'nine tails is his least favorite method of redirection, so those stripes he shall earn."

"Allah's ways?" Master Emine's soft voice sounded hard through the rock walls. "Sirs, while the Sultan may find your methods productive, I can assure you that one cannot whip knowledge into a pupil. One must, instead, cultivate a distinct love of learning so that knowledge and understanding takes root."

Neither captor answered.

"Like seeds planted in the field," Master Emine continued, as though the guards were the pupils.

From the other side of the wall, Vlad imagined his tutor's hands gesticulating, as they always did when he became impassioned about what he was teaching.

"The planter cannot beat the seeds with a trowel every morning and expect them to sprout. Instead, the wise planter must nurture his seeds. Water them and provide them sunshine. Pull the weeds. Then the seed will grow and bear fruit." He paused to let his point sink in. "Beating the seed only serves to produce bad fruits. Or kills the seed before it can sprout at all. Now if you gentlemen will excuse me."

Vlad's heart swelled with emotion as Master Emine retreated, his footfalls padding away, down the corridor of the castle.

*Thank you, God, for one friend.*

Ahmed's voice was a low growl. "If Emine was not the Sultan's favorite wife's brother, he would already be dead for such blasphemous talk."

After the conversation in the hallway, Master Emine paid special attention to Vlad, who was noticeably thinner and paler than the rest of the Wallachian boys. All seven resided in the dungeon for failing to submit, but it was Vlad who took the brunt of all punishment.

Master Emine must have known this, because he praised him for his scholastic accomplishments and smiled when their eyes met. He instructed the other boys to listen when Vlad spoke, because as he said, when Vlad spoke, the words that passed his lips were worth listening to.

*A true leader*, Master Emine had repeated several times. *Vlad Drăculea is a name that will be forever remembered for the way his mind works.*

Linguistics and philosophy were subjects in which Vlad excelled, and in Persian, Emine meant trustworthy. Vlad figured his tutor's mother had aptly named her son, because Master Emine had proven himself to be just that. Trustworthy. Even to a lowly political prisoner such as himself.

Doing as his beloved tutor requested, Vlad stood up from his overstuffed pillow chair as Master Emine began to clap. Radu, face brighter than the rest of the boys, joined in almost at once. The other boys followed suit until raucous clapping thundered in the small study. For the first time since coming to Tokat, something lifted in his chest.

The Ottoman guards, who never allowed Vlad to venture too far from their grasp, exchanged a look but obediently did as Master Emine said and clapped for Vlad. From the corner of his eye, however, Vlad could see that whilst their hands clapped, their faces were shadowed with hatred.

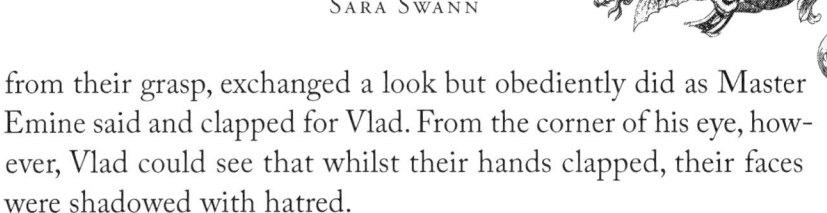

Vlad ignored them. With everyone clapping and his tutor grinning, he almost smiled, too.

Almost.

Two Turks, each in flowing robes and turbans, stepped silently into the study and whispered quietly to Ahmed. Vlad watched from the corner of his eye as Ahmed listened and nodded. A wicked grin cracked his long, pointed face into almost inhuman planes.

Without waiting for the clapping to die down, Ahmed nodded to his beady-eyed counterpart. Like thieves, they hulked over and each grabbed Radu by an arm.

"Hey!" The bright smile melted from Radu's round face as his eyes transformed from sparkling to terrified. "Let me go!"

Grinning, they dragged Radu to the door.

His terrified voice sang out in a wailing cry. "*Frate*! Vlad! *Ajuța*, help me!"

Vlad dove to grab Radu from their grasp, but Ahmed stepped in his path. Vlad crashed into the large Turk, who may as well have been a wall instead of a man.

"Sirs, please, allow the child to continue his studies," Master Emine begged. "This is not sophisticated nor is it dignified!"

Vlad reached around Ahmed but was unable feel Radu at all.

Ahmed spat on him and gave him a shove. "Stupid non-believer."

Vlad tumbled back onto his pillow chair.

"Emine," Ahmed scolded, "mind your duties and we will mind ours." He paused at the door and cast a black glare at the Ottoman tutor. "Or else."

Radu and the two captors disappeared into the maze of hallways.

"Radu! Remain strong!" Vlad's voice strangled in his throat as he fought the fluff of the pillow. He prayed nobody heard the crack in his voice. "I will find you!"

"Vlad!" Though he could no longer see his younger brother, the hopeless tone in Radu's tone echoed in the dank hall.

By the time he fought his way out of his pillow chair, Radu's voice was no more. Vlad stood helplessly behind the closed door. His shoulders sagged.

*Today is the last time I will see my little brother.* The tiny voice in the back of Vlad's mind refused to be silenced. *You are now alone, Vlad. Alone in the court of the devil himself.*

Master Emine's voice was softer than usual. "Perhaps we should suspend tutoring for today."

Vlad shook his head. "No, pray continue Master Emine."

Master Emine complied, though Vlad heard nothing more of the rich knowledge his beloved tutor imparted—not that day nor any of the days that followed.

†††

"Prince Vlad." The words reverberated in Vlad's hollow mind, a mind wracked with exhaustion and hunger. The voice sounded otherworldly against the dungeon walls. His body ached, and the whip marks from the cat o'nine tails were raw and painfully tender. He groaned.

Again, he had been dragged to the Sultan's room.

Again, he had resisted and fought against the advances of the men. Again, his resistance proved futile. Again, he was overpowered.

Again, he refused to submit.

*I will never give in. Never.*

"Prince Vlad, please listen."

Vlad groaned and willed the fuzziness to leave his head.

"Prince Vlad?"

Vlad recognized Luca's voice. His fellow Wallachian resistor always called him prince and seemed a willing subject. Even here, in this unimaginable hell, and despite Vlad's inability to protect him, or anybody else.

"Luca?" Vlad groaned again. "Yes?"

"It is about Radu. He submitted."

Vlad's foggy mind snapped to attention. "You mean Radu is not here?"

Luca was quiet for a moment, as if willing himself to summon up the courage to break bad news to Vlad. "He will never be here again, Prince."

Vlad's hands began to shake so that his shackles rattled. "How do you know this?"

Luca paused again before daring to speak. "They came for me after they took you. Rest assured I did not submit, Prince. Like you, I will fight these wretched devils until I die."

"A true Wallachian. And I will remember your fierce loyalty when we get out of here."

Luca must have adjusted in the darkness because his chains rattled, then stopped. "As they dragged me through the halls, I saw him. I saw Radu."

"How did you find him?"

"He was at prayer, Prince. Face down on a mat, facing Mecca."

The power of speech was as far from Vlad as was the safety of his family's Wallachian castle. A tiny gasp strangled in his throat.

"I wish I had better news to present to you, Prince." Luca's voice was ringed with a truly apologetic tone. "But he was dressed in jewels and royal robes, too. He was with Mehmed, the Sultan's son. Since he submitted, he has a room in the castle. He will never be down here with the likes of us again."

Minutes passed, minutes that slowly turned into hours. Silence filled the miserable, musty dungeon, heavy, like a storm cloud.

Finally, Vlad spoke. "No matter what happens Luca, resist. You are a fine Wallachian. I will not ever forget you. I will make certain you get out of these walls."

†††

"Dinner time." The Turk's keys jangled as he strode through the open door.

The Wallachian boys in chains squinted into the intrusive light.

"Shackles up," he instructed.

A collective groan rose from the lot of them as the broken, battered boys did as they were told and held out their hands to be unlocked.

Vlad squinted against the light but did not groan as the others. Instead, he studied the guard who, unlike the guards on the previous nights who came in pairs to unlock them for the evening meal, came alone.

*Fat fool.*

Vlad sniffed the air. The scent of spiced brandy hung about his person as a condemned man hung about the gallows.

*He is drunk.*

The plan almost laid itself before him. When the guard, humming a drunken tune, came to unlock his chains, Vlad did The Sign of the Cross in Romanian.

În numele Tatălui, și al Fiului, și al Sfântului Duh. Amin.

*Father, forgive me for failing You. I failed to protect my little brother from the godless heathens who are our captors. In light of my failure, Radu turned his back on me, on our country, and most importantly and most unforgivably, on You. Help me, Father, as I make flight through this hellish country from captivity to the safety of Wallachia. Amin.*

The guard scoffed as he unlocked Vlad's chains. "Such silly superstition. Ignorant non-believer."

As the scoffing guard leaned down to unlock him, he fumbled the key and dropped it into the rotting hay. "Oops," he giggled.

Vlad rolled his eyes. "Inept fool," he muttered.

"What did you—"

As the guard raised up, having retrieved the elusive key, Vlad grasped his hands together so that he, too, could be unlocked. Once the key clicked in the lock, Vlad swung his arms at the Turk's face like a club. The drunken guard sank to his knees.

The other boys gasped and began to murmur loudly.

Thinking fast, Vlad brought up a knee to his jailer's chin and heard something in the Turk's face crack. He fell sideways, like a dead tree in a windstorm. Vlad ran over him easily.

Before his senses had a chance to catch up with him, Vlad was out the door and running through the hallways that he had been forcefully dragged through so many times.

*Only a few more turns and I will be safe under the cover of the falling darkness.*

Aches and pains from the various beatings and assaults did nothing to slow him, but instead spurred him onward, down the halls, and into the unfamiliar territory outside the castle walls. Tears streamed from his eyes as he ran.

*Blessed Mother Mary, pray for me in the hour of my death. Which may be lurking behind Turkish bushes tonight.*

*Amin.*

# Capitol Şase

*Târgovişte Castle, Wallachia*
*in the Year of our Lord, 1443*

*His speech was smooth as butter, yet war was in his heart;*
*His words were softer than oil, yet they were drawn swords.*
*~Psalm 55:21*

My Brother in Christ and Fellow Leader of Christendom John Hunyadi of Transylvania:

*Greetings from the throne of Wallachia, your friend and ally against the ever-present threat of Ottoman Invasion. My boyars tell me that a letter was intercepted by your camp that was meant for Sultan Mehmed and that, in light of my wording in said letter, my fellow Christians think me to have sided with our shared enemy, the Ottoman Empire.*

*Rest assured that I have done what I think best for peace in my realm, since Wallachia is the only land lying between the Ottoman Empire and your beloved Transylvania.*

*Rest assured that I have broken peace with the Ottoman Empire since resuming my rightful throne by dealing with Christian kingdoms such as yours in a friendly manner and, in doing so, have betrayed two innocent souls—Vlad III and Radu Drăculea.*

*Please understand that I have allowed my children to be butchered for the sake of Christian peace, in order that both I and my country might continue to be vassals of the Holy Roman Emperor.*

*Yours in Christ,*

*Vlad Drăculea II, King of Wallachia and Defender of the Faith*

†††

Mircea read over his father's shoulder as he poked his quill pen back into the inkwell. Normally, Mircea liked to listen as his father wrote letters. The familiar *scratch-scratch-scratch* of the quill across the thick paper was somehow soothing, as was the smell of the fresh ink as it soaked into the paper. Comforting. Like the soft memory of an oft-sung nursery rhyme in a moment of darkness. But there was nothing comforting in this letter—scratching of the quill or not—nor any of those that came before it.

"Father, that letter . . ."

Vlad II stared, once again, into the candle's flame that burned beneath the wax ladle. "Hmm?"

Mircea cocked an eyebrow. "Well, it is almost an exact replica of the one you sent to Sultan Murad II, only in this draft, you play the other side." Mircea swallowed hard before he continued. "And those ghastly things you said about Vlad III and Radu . . ."

The king sat back and twitched his moustache. Mircea was not quite sure how his father managed to stiffen it to such an extreme point, but he did. And he never shared his secret of how he did so, either. He blew on the ink, then folded the letter with severe creases just has he had the letter to the Sultan. Over two ribbons in the royal colors, he poured the bubbling purple wax and affixed his seal. "Since when is the truth ghastly?"

Mircea's heart dropped in his chest, seemingly all the way down to his stomach. "You mean, Vlad and Radu are—dead? By the Sultan's hand?"

The Voivode shrugged nonchalantly. "I broke our agreement. I swore an oath to Sultan Murad that I would side with the

Ottoman Empire should they invade Hungary or Transylvania or even Wallachia."

"Father!" Mircea shook his head as though that would make the words somehow transform into something less ghastly. "You did *what*?"

Mircea's father paid his interruption absolutely no mind. Some days, Vlad II would become killing mad over such an interruption as this. Other days, apparently like today, he simply ignored them.

Vlad II continued. "They invaded Transylvania, just as they said they would. The Ottomans you see, they kept their word. Just as I did when I did not halt their progress into the land of Christendom. I promised if they did just as they did, that I would defend them. However, when they crossed the Danube, I double-crossed them."

Mircea stood in stark silence. "What was it that changed your mind then?"

"I thought of my sons, I truly did. Had I kept the truce with the Ottomans, your brothers would be safe. However, until at the last moment when I chose to side with John Hunyadi, I had failed to think of all the souls of all the Christians lost in this escapade from that day forward, those are souls I will stand in Judgement for when Christ comes back. And If I did not stand up for them, I would certainly burn for eternity."

Mircea stared at his father in horror.

Vlad II continued. "I did not hold up my oath to the Ottomans," he repeated, as if saying it the first time was not terrible enough, "and those were the terms, clearly laid out, that we both agreed to. That if I broke our agreement, Vlad and Radu were his to do with as he saw fit. Or to dispose of appropriately."

"Dispose of?"

"Had I sided with the Ottomans, at least Vlad would be on his way back to Wallachia. Radu's fate was always questionable . . ."

"Father! Really!" Mircea was aghast. His stomach turned over, and he feared he would vomit all over his father and his atrocious desk. "They are our *blood!*"

Vlad II plucked his seal out of the hardened wax and motioned for a groomsman, who took the letter away at once. "No, boy. Vlad and Radu, they are simply pawns in a great game of chess, where the rules are everchanging, and nobody knows who writes them." He shifted his gaze momentarily from the flame to Mircea. "As are you."

Mircea backed up a step. A cold chill coursed over his flesh and left goosebumps in its wake, as though Death himself had just trailed a finger down his very backbone. For a fleeting moment, he found himself wishing he had incurred his father's wrath with his abrupt words instead of his apparent apathy.

There was something haunting in his words, but Mircea could not be certain whether he was heartsick over Radu and Vlad's demise at the Ottomans' hands, or over the fact that his beloved, flickering candle was burned down to a nub.

"Yes, you three sons of mine are nothing but pawns." Vlad II looked back into the flame. "As am I." His voice went from icy to defeated in a matter of syllables. "Nobody knows the future, Mircea. Nobody even knows the rules by which we play. Nor do they know who wins, how the winner is determined, or who loses. Who lives. Who dies." Vlad II sighed and pinched the candleflame between his thumb and forefinger. "We are all just—pawns."

# Capitol Şapte

Tokat Castle, Turkey
in the Year of our Lord, 1443

*Though I walk through the valley of the shadow of death,
I will fear no evil: For Thou art with me.*

~Psalm 23:4

The morning star was deceptively innocent and bright when Vlad, still half asleep against the base of a rocky outcropping in the middle of enemy territory, the Ottoman Empire, heard it—the whuffing sound of grazing camels.

Had he been more awake, it would have been a warning.

A warning to run.

A warning to hide.

A warning to take cover.

But he was not more awake. The warning came too late.

Gruff hands closed around Vlad's thin arms and yanked him to his feet so quickly he was unable to stay upright on his own accord. Those angry hands, however, ensured he remained standing.

The white robe of the Persians he had been forced to wear as a political prisoner at Tokat Castle was torn and muddy from his arduous, nighttime journey through the Turkish desert. His feet, cut and bloody from running without sandals, threatened to betray him as he stood on shaky knees. The chill from the long night and the exhausted tremble in his muscles sapped the fight from him before it had the chance to bloom, and his vision wavered in the early morning dawn as the world around him refused to come into focus.

Ahmed's face, pinched and somehow proud, came into focus, and Vlad knew in that moment he had stumbled into the direst of straits. Ahmed's lips tilted into a sardonic smile.

"*Salaam alaikum*, Prince." He drew back his hand and slapped Vlad's cold cheek with a vengeance. "You truly are a stupid imbecile. To think, a lowly prisoner such as yourself, believing that he has the authority to leave the Sultan's castle on your own whim!"

Ahmed slapped him again and, this time, let him fall to the ground in a crumpled heap.

Vlad coughed and sputtered in the dirt. His feet cramped, and coppery blood pooled in his mouth. "Get him on a camel," Ahmed barked. "Tie him down. The prince will pay for his indiscretions."

Unseen hands snatched Vlad from the bloody ground and hefted him onto one of the waiting camels, stomach down, between the humps. He shifted his weight as leather thongs bit into the tender skin of his wrists and ankles. Once he was sufficiently tied, someone cinched his binds tight and pulled his hands and feet together beneath the stomach of the camel. Vlad gasped as the air was squeezed out of him. He tried to take in another breath, but from this angle, it was incredibly difficult, bordering on impossible.

"He will pay, yes," a disembodied voice, probably the cincher, agreed, "but in all honesty, who would have counted on him making it this far?"

Ahmed's voice was sharp. "Nothing that hints at a compliment regarding this non-believer shall ever pass your blasphemous lips again." He paused. "Or I'll cut them off and serve them to the Sultan on a platter wrapped in Baghdad silk."

"You threaten your equal in such a manner?" the voice was incredulous.

"You are not my equal."

The immaterial voice spoke again, but in a more muted tone. "Then I suppose I should consider myself warned."

Vlad listened to the exchange but did not make a sound. The camel's sharp backbone pressed into his stomach making it hurt to take any sort of breath, deep or shallow. He tried to adjust, but it was futile. Instead, he pictured Ahmed's face, contorted into a grimace in the heavy silence.

"Threatened?" Ahmed *tsked* in the back of his throat. "No. You are *promised*."

Vlad's concealed captor must have wanted to keep his lips, because not another word was spoken until the caravan of camels was turned and headed back to Tokat Castle. Then, it was only Ahmed who spoke.

"Young fool. I give you no marks for bravery as you, unprepared as you were, simply ran yourself to exhaustion and had no provisions to sustain yourself. To show for it, you were caught."

Vlad listened but did not dare give Ahmed ammunition against him. He need not know the innerworkings of Vlad's mind. How he was careful to stick to the river to have a water source without having to lug it along with him in a pouch he certainly did not have at his disposal. Or that he had picked tubers from the soil and fruits from the scrubby bushes. Not just any fruits, but only the ones that he saw the birds eat. No, death certainly was not going to come to him in the form of starvation or dehydration. The only threats to his freedom, besides Ahmed, had proven to be time itself—and distance.

"You do not even know how far it is to your precious Târgovişte." A camel quirt smacked him, sharp, across his bottom. He was helpless to retaliate, being bound to the camel such as he was. "You are a month away from your beloved Târgovişte, Prince. To get home, you must cross an ocean and a country where you are considered the enemy. And you, fool that you are, thought you could make the journey alone."

SARA SWANN

*Smack!*

Tears sprang to Vlad's eyes. He had run all night from Tokat Castle and put considerable distance between that hellish place and his person. Now, he would have to endure the ride back not only in agony, but also in humiliation. His tattered, dirty robe did not prove to be much protection against the camel quirt.

He expected more whips as the trip wore on, but none came. It was as though Ahmed was toying with him. Vlad was powerless, and they both knew it.

After some time of riding in silence, Ahmed's voice came again. "You may think this to be your punishment, child. But again, you are wrong. Your punishment is coming, in fact, it has not even begun. The last boy who tried to run away . . ." He let his words hang there, haunting and cruel.

*Is Ahmed somehow reading my mind?*

In case the elder Turk truly did know how to read minds, Vlad took great care to keep his thoughts stoic.

*I will fear no evil for thou art with me.*

"The lions," Ahmed continued. "I know you have heard them roar."

*Thy rod and thy staff, they comfort me.*

Ahmed belched. "They ate very well when we returned to the castle. With the last boy who tried to run away, that is."

*Thou makest me to lie down beside the still waters.*

"Rest assured, your punishment for this transgression will be worse than a thousand deaths."

*Thou preparest a table before me in the presence of mine enemies; Thou anointest my head with oil; my cup runneth over.*

"You will see." Ahmed let go a cruel chuckle but spoke no more. Heavy silence, however, was their constant companion all the way back to Tokat.

†††

"See that there, in the distance?" Ahmed's cutting voice roused Vlad from an uneasy sleep. His head pounded from being bent over the camel and muscles in strange places burned and pulled.

"Oh, I forgot. Lowly you can see nothing except the underside of this camel. What you do *not* see is Tokat Castle."

Vlad's bladder ached, and his feet knotted in righteous cramps.

"Ride ahead and tell the Sultan I am approaching with the prisoner. And he is ready for his punishment."

Several minutes passed before Vlad dared turn his head and peek at his surroundings. Bending his neck hurt his head, but the feeling of relief that washed over him at seeing the rock walls around the mouth of the palace's cave entrance proved to be an odd emotion.

*The ride is over.*

A feeling of failure quickly replaced any sense of relief that may or may not be coming.

When they reached the castle, Ahmed took his time cutting the straps that bound Vlad to the camel. Instead of hastening to release him, Ahmed took care first to urinate, then to stretch. When he finally cut the straps, Vlad, his young body almost completely numb, slid off the camel and landed in the dirt with a thud.

"Are you ready for your punishment, Prince?" Ahmed towered over him. "Because it is about to be exacted upon you."

Ahmed made no move to help Vlad stand on his numb legs, but instead stood idly by as Vlad tried to stand, fell, then tried again.

Vlad's young bladder, swollen and stretched from the ride, threatened to revolt if he did not relieve it soon. The sudden addition of a woman's screams, so incredibly out of place in the dull, Turkish morning, drew Vlad's attention from his aching body to the mouth of the cave.

The woman, big with child and dressed in flowing, royal robes, shrieked behind Sultan Murad and matched his quick pace, which appeared awkward and painful due to her considerable size, as he strode out of the mouth of the cave. *The secret entrance that Radu and I accidentally discovered.*

During his time at Tokat, Vlad had become fluent in Turkish, and easily picked up her hysterical words. Words that chilled his blood.

*Stop.*
*Please.*
*Mercy.*
*Do not do this.*
*Do not hurt the children.*

Confused, Vlad thought, *Children? But it was only me who ran...*

Unsure of what exactly was happening, Vlad stared at the scene as it unfolded before him. The sharp-nosed Sultan reached the center of the courtyard ande turned to face him.

"You did this, Prince," Sultan Murad bellowed. "You did this to them when you chose to insult my leniency. When you attempted to run away!"

*Them?*

Vision fuzzy and head still throbbing, Vlad, half bent over, squinted at the Sultan. Another man in white had joined him, and in his grasp were two of his dungeon-mates, each of them gagged and bloody. Vlad smacked his hands over his eyes and rubbed hard.

*God, no. Please, do not let this be happening.*

When Vlad opened his eyes, the sight that lay before him had not changed. Helpless and writhing in Sultan Murad's grasp were his two of his fellow Wallachian resistors.

"Luca!" Vlad yelled. "Andrei!" He started toward them, but in his hunched and hobbling state, Ahmed was able to knock him easily to the ground.

Luca and Andrei gurgled incoherently from behind the gags that filled their mouths. Their bulging eyes, made even wider with fear, locked on Vlad's.

Pleading. Terrified. Begging for a help that was not and never had been in his power to provide.

"Sultan," the pregnant woman shrieked, "you are my husband and my head, but please, do this not!"

Murad waved his hand as though doing nothing more than shooing a bothersome fly. "Away, Woman!"

The Sultan's dismissal of his youngest wife brought her hysterical shrieks to an even higher octave. When the sultan's henchmen appeared in their flowing robes to pull her away, Vlad half expected her, in her present state, to reach for Murad's curved sword and snatch it from his belt. Somewhere in his mind, he wished she would.

*Only one ally, just one ally, and we could change the trajectory here and now, for the better. Please, woman, be my ally.*

The Sultan, unmoved by the wailing woman, snatched the whimpering boys by their collars and gave them each a hearty shake. "You watch this punishment, Prince, as it has been constructed especially for your eyes. Remember, as they are, soon shall *you* be! As are you now—" He stared hard at Vlad. "So once were they."

*If I could just get up and get over there . . .*

Ahmed struck him, hard, against the side of his head with what felt like a stick. "Acknowledge the Sultan!"

The world tilted in his vision before righting itself. However, before Vlad could muster any semblance of an answer, the Sultan yelled again. "Bring forth the knotted rope!"

*No!*

On all fours and with fuzzy vision, Vlad attempted to crawl across the dirt, but another crashing blow from Ahmed—this time hard against the small of his back—stilled him.

Before he could figure any sort of plan, to Vlad's absolute horror, two robed men with hard faces appeared beside the Sultan. From each of their hands hung a knotted rope.

At the sight of the men, Luca began to kick and fight against his gag, his eyes wide with terror.

One of the grinning, robed men sporting a rope overpowered him easily. He looped the rope around Luca's head, with the knots of the ropes pressed into his eyes. Vlad's heartbeat quickened to a gallop as the stomach-churning scene continued to unfold, but he was powerless to look away.

Groan after pitiful, heartbreaking groan roiled forth from Luca's throat as the nameless man held the rope, and a second robed man looped his rope around Andrei's eyes.

"You did this, Prince Vlad Drăculea of Wallachia," the Sultan cried. "You did this to these two young Wallachian men."

"Then take me," Vlad's voice wavered. "If I am to blame as you say, take me!"

"I shall not spill royal blood. Know you nothing of the law?" Sultan Murad made a slicing motion with his hand, as though ordering a beheading.

In tandem, the robed men tightened the ropes against the boys' eyes until Andrei's cries, muffled by the gag, joined Luca's in a choir of anguish and suffering. Punctuated by Murad's laughter, Luca's shrieks reached an excruciating crescendo, before melting away into a whimper. Through tear-bleary eyes, Vlad stared at Luca, watching the bloody goo seeped out from beneath the knots that, Vlad knew, had taken the sight of his only loyal friend.

Ahmed looked down at Vlad. An evil laugh escaped his lips. "Sultan! The non-believer urinated on himself! Such a female, you are."

Vlad sniffled to the tune of raucous laughter that came from everywhere. It was not until that moment that he felt the hot wetness on his thighs. Sure enough, during the Sultan's horrific display, his overfilled bladder had let go. A single tear escaped its lashy dam and tracked down his cheek. The robed men dropped Luca and Andrei, ropes still knotted about their heads, in a pitiful, bloody heap.

"They will be no longer be my prisoners. They are now slaves." The Sultan's voice was cool—no, cold. Like a viper. "Or better yet, take them back to the dungeon. If the young prince still refuses to cooperate, feed them both to the lions."

Ahmed spoke as Vlad, open mouthed, stared at his fellow countrymen. "What do you want me to do with *him*?"

The Sultan turned his back on the whole scene and swaggered

back toward the cave entrance. Howling moans from his youngest wife, somewhere nearby but out of sight, set the entire gruesome scene to music.

Vlad wondered, for a brief moment, if she was wracked with birth pains or pains of sorrow for the young Wallachian boys who would never see another sunset. Never see their homeland. Never see—anything, ever again, nothing at all.

The Sultan paused before entering the cave and spoke over his shoulder. "Leave him."

"Leave him?" Ahmed's voice was incredulous. "After he ran away?"

"If he disobeys, we feed the boys to the lions. Their deaths will be on his conscious, which is already heavy with the suffering which he alone inflicted upon his fellow Wallachians. Come, Ahmed, let us eat."

Vlad began to shake as he watched them walk together, laughing and joking, into the castle. The two nameless brutes who had blinded Luca and Andrei grabbed them with unfeeling hands and dragged them away, ignoring their whimpers as easily as a lion would ignore the bleats of a helpless sheep.

"Welcome to the mindset of a ruler, Prince," the Sultan called from the cave's entrance. "Remember, *you* did that to Luca and Andrei."

Vlad sat in the urine-soaked mud, head down.

Alone.

Trembling.

Hungry.

Hurting.

Before he could think of what to do, where to go, or of anything at all, an image of the Blessed Mother, beautiful in her white veil and heavenly blue mantle, filled his mind. He wanted so much to hug her, to curl up in her lap as he was sure Jesus had done as a child. Since her husband, Joseph, was a carpenter, Vlad was certain he had made Mary a rocking chair. Perhaps she rocked Jesus to sleep as he had rocked Radu and as their governess had rocked him.

*Oh, Blessed Mother, look at what I have done.*

Her calming presence and gentle smile made his blood warm within his veins. Not the way Ahmed's presence made his blood boil—but warm. Like when he would wrap himself and Radu in the wooly quilt Grandmother Mara knitted for him for his first Christmastide.

*It is probably draped over the rocking chair in my old nursery right now.*

Mother Mary's presence stayed with him—possibly for minutes; perhaps for hours. With the warmth in his blood, he somehow felt stronger. More hopeful. For absolutely no reason other than the Blessed Mother came to spend time with him in his hour of need.

*God says to forgive, Mother Mary, but I can never forgive him. Any of them.*

Despite Vlad's brutal honesty about his obvious shortcoming with the Queen of Heaven and Earth, still, she stayed with him like a good mother would stay with her brokenhearted child.

The sun already made haste toward the horizon before Vlad felt well enough to stand, and it was well below the horizon when he felt able to make the trek back into the prison of Tokat Castle. Without fighting or even saying a word to any of the wall-like Turks that stared at him, Vlad held his chin high and limped down the pristine halls all the way to the dungeon.

*His* dungeon.

As he waited for the guard to open the door, Vlad thought he caught the sound of a wailing woman echoing off the walls, like a nightmare that refused to be extinguished by the dawn.

# viii

## Capitol Opt

### Tokat Castle, Turkey
### in the Year of our Lord, 1447

*Whoever is patient has great understanding,*
*But one who is quick-tempered displays folly.*
*~Proverbs 14:29*

D*earest Vlad,*
*Years have passed since I have last seen your face, and I miss your dark hair and kind eyes. I long for the day when I might gaze upon them again, in the early dawn or the falling twilight, as I was blessed to do so many times before.*

Ioana's words met his ears, and Vlad thought he was dreaming. He could almost hear the musical Grecian lilt to her words. Almost.

*I pray you are being treated well and the time passes quickly until you are able to return to your rightful home. You mentioned in your last letter that you had taken a trip north to see some of the Ottoman countryside. Pray tell me, what is it like? Is it a beautiful wonderland, the likes of which the world has never seen?*

A chorus of masculine laughter roused Vlad from his sleep. Through bleary eyes, he could just make out Ahmed, reading from a letter in a mockingly feminine voice, flanked by two other robed Turks.

"Beautiful wonderland?" one scoffed.

"Is that really how the non-believer sees life here in the dungeon?" the other joined.

The three of them jeered loudly.

Vlad glanced around the dungeon, which was brightly lit thanks to the dungeon door leading into the castle having been left open. Wallachian eyes, saddened by what was happening to their prince, gazed at Vlad.

"A letter, my letter?" The words fairly tumbled off his tongue into the stark realization of what was happening.

Ahmed ignored him, cleared his throat, and continued to read.

*I trust they are educating you well, since you are a royal Wallachian and entitled to such an education. I would love to hear of all the likes of which you are learning.*

"What is it you are learning, Prince?" Ahmed shifted his eyes and stared hotly at Vlad. "Anything you would like to share with this little love interest of yours? Perhaps of what happens in the Sultan's chambers?"

The trio of captors laughed once again, an evil laugh that echoed off the dungeon walls.

Vlad pushed himself to his feet, half expecting to be stopped by the ever-present chains that wrapped about his wrists and ankles. He glanced down.

*How odd is it that my chains are unlocked?* he thought.

*I had that dream the other night, the one I have spoken of to you before. You and I, out catching licurici by moonlight, when our hands met for the first time. You pulled me close and cupped my face with your hand. Our lips met. I knew in that moment I had experienced the first kiss of my life with the only man I ever wanted to kiss, and that is still true. I did not want that moment to end and I long for the day when you return.*

*I am faithfully waiting for you, Vlad.*
*All my love,*
*Ioana*

Every eye in the dungeon shifted from Ahmed to Vlad, who stood with fists knotted at his side.

"Give me my letter."

Ahmed sneered as he slowly folded the precious paper back along its creases. Careful not to break eye contact, he brought the letter to his lips and kissed it before tucking it into his robe. "Perhaps I shall invite this virginal woman of yours for a visit to Tokat. To visit me. Not you."

Vlad took a step towards the three captors, who stood ready to intercept him.

"Prince, stop!" Luca's shouting voice caught Vlad off guard, and he did stop.

Though he could no longer see, Luca and Andrei had apparently been brought in for this heartless display, as they sat together in the corner. After their blinding, they were kept within the walls of the castle, presumably as slaves, but more likely just to be kept out of Vlad's sight so he would behave, on pain of their deaths.

"It is a trap," Luca continued.

Ahmed's simper melted from his angular face. "Ah, now your loyal subject has ruined the fun. He will pay for that later." He drew his thin lips back in a sneer. "After I make this Ioana one of my wives. Or one of my concubines."

Vlad's vision tinged to a fiery red. Before he could stop himself, he rushed Ahmed, who was obviously not expecting the young Wallachian to do so. Vlad's fist flew on its own, and he landed one hit to the side of Ahmed's face, before a crushing blow from an unseen Turk sent him tumbling backward and shrouded his world in darkness once again.

When Vlad awoke, dried blood had tightened the skin of his face. He rubbed his eyes, but nothing would come into focus. *Perhaps it is just dark.*

The jingling of keys was followed by a piercing ray of light from the castle door. There, in the doorway, loomed Ahmed. His form was fuzzy, but Vlad could just make out a supremely swollen jaw and blackened eye. He almost smiled to himself.

Ahmed, however, simply patted his robe where he had stored Ioana's letter. Anger renewed afresh; Vlad lunged at his heartless captor. Something stopped him, and he fell to the ground.

*They have chained me to the wall by my ankles. Like a beast.*

Vlad pushed himself to his feet, but he may as well have been standing on blocks of bloodless wood. He fell again.

From the doorway, Ahmed laughed and pulled the door closed, cloaking the silent Wallachian boys and their brokenhearted prince in darkness once again.

From that day forward, whenever the door opened Vlad fought like the beast they forced him to become. Like a chained tiger when the men would come and try and take him for themselves or to the Sultan's chambers. Like a wild wolf whenever they came to unlock him for tutoring. Like a mad lion when someone appeared to unlock him for dinner. He fought so hard, that Vlad began having more meals alone, chained in the dungeon, than in the dining hall with the rest of the captives.

Though he continued to resist, Vlad was careful not to anger the guards to the point of murder. The thought was there, ever-present in his mind, with the images of Luca and Andrei.

*Should they tire of trying to break me, it will not be me they kill . . .*

†††

*Lord have mercy. Christ have mercy. Lord have mercy.*

Vlad let the chants roll up from his chest and off his tongue. The words reverberated off the rock walls and sounded vaguely like his old rock church back home in Wallachia, where the chants of the priest and gathered Catholics would intermingle in the cool of the morning celebration of Mass and the Latin words would hang in the air and cloak him, and everyone, like a loving garment of safety and security.

## DEFENDER OF THE FAITH

The image of Sabbas the Goth, a Wallachian from the third century and celebrated Saint from Târgoviște, popped into Vlad's mind.

*They called you the Mad Martyr—a man so in love with Christ, he could not wait to give his life in his Savior's honor. Saint Sabbas the Goth, from my Wallachia, you never denounced your Christian faith, and you welcomed death in the face of your torturers—the Goths—who felt you betrayed them and their pagan ways by following Christ.*

*You chose to go hungry as you refused to eat the meat they sacrificed to idols. You stood up for what was right and denounced what was wrong. When asked in public by those who meant to persecute any who chose to follow Christ, "Who among you is a Christian," you were so beloved that your fellow Wallachians sought to hide you and your faith in an attempt to keep you safe. However, you chose to proudly follow Jesus, and strode into their midst, your head high, and proclaimed your faith for all of heaven and earth to hear.*

*When they beat you, you blessed them. When they tied you to the Breaking Wheel, you excitedly proclaimed that you felt no pain and your Savior was to thank for it. Still, pagan women and your fellow countrymen tried to save your earthly life by untying you from the wheel in the dead of night, but still, you refused to escape, choosing instead to stay so that you might take your earthly punishment for living a life like Jesus, and ultimately claim your eternal reward.*

*When they took you to the Mussovo River outside of Târgoviște to drown you, again your captors—seeing no evil in you—set you free. You begged them to do their job, as you were strong in your faith and you did not want them to meet the same fate as you for failing to carry out their orders.*

*You saw Saints waiting to accept your soul on the far riverbank, and you met your earthly death happily and with a smile.*

*Saint Sabbas, my brother Radu, whom I have failed to protect, has turned his back on God, the Faith, and on me in exchange for a lenient life at the court of our captors, the court of our enemies. He has male lovers, female lovers, and is the favourite of the sometimes Sultan, Mehmed, himself. Everything about this hellish place is an abomination and a mockery in the face of God. Why must I remain a prisoner here, when my reason for being here—to protect Radu from their heathen clutches—is no more? Radu has forsaken me.*

*Lend me your strength, fellow Wallachian. Fellow Christian. Fellow Soldier of God.*

"Come, Prince." Ahmed's mocking voice interrupted his prayer.

Vlad had been so engrossed in his prayers, that he had failed to hear the castle door to the dungeon creak open.

Ahmed placed a hand on his shoulder, more gently than ever before. Vlad shuddered and shrugged infinitesimally.

"You know your prayers are in vain, in any language. Recognize Allah as your god, and your faith will be richly rewarded."

The memory of the pitiful, broken boys, Luca and Andrei, who suffered for simply being Wallachian, came to mind. If Vlad incited too much of Ahmed's anger, their lives would be lost. Horrifically. He had not seen either of them since the day of the letter fiasco. "Tell me, Ahmed, how do Luca and Andrei?"

Ahmed's hand, which had fluttered above his shoulder with his shrug, fell back onto his bony shoulder. His grip tightened like a vice. "You think I have not kept my word to you. You think I have killed them. You dare call me a liar!"

Vlad did not bother to respond. There was no use. Any of his words could be twisted, and Ahmed was the master at doing so. With only a simple, harmless question, he managed to anger the most volatile and dangerous of his captors.

"Stupid child. You stand at the feet of faith and refuse to accept it." Ahmed refused to relax his grip and gave Vlad's shoulder a shake. "Come. It is time for your tutoring."

By the time they arrived at the study where Master Emine stood, beaming, Vlad's shoulder ached from Ahmed's iron grip. Master Emine reached for Vlad's hand and pulled him from Ahmed's grasp. "Ah, Prince. Please, take your seat at the head of the class."

Blood returned to Vlad's arm with a welcome tingle. He flickered as much of a smile as he could manage at his tutor before daring a glance around the room. Radu no longer came since accepting a place at court, and because of this, in this world, he was now considered of a much, much higher status than the likes of them.

Nicolai and Măriuca sat, backs impossibly straight, at the oval table, but dared not glance at him.

In the corner, huddled together, sat Luca and Andrei. Vlad's heart lightened at once.

*Thank you, God. They are alive.*

One Wallachian, however, was missing. Questions had not proven to be the best course of action so far this morning, still Vlad could not help but inquire after the absent Wallachian. Somehow, he felt responsible for all the Romanian boys. "Master Emine, how is Ștefan?"

Emine's smile stiffened. "He joined the ranks of your brother, Prince Vlad."

"I see." Vlad tried to keep his words from seething, but he failed.

*God, forgive me for not protecting yet another of my countrymen.*

Master Emine tapped his baton on the oval desk. "Let us begin, pupils. Where were we last time? Ah yes, the maths of Pythagoras."

The door to the study creaked open. A square-faced Persian stuck his head inside and whispered something in Turkish. Vlad strained to listen.

"The Sultan and his wives—they have gone on to Constantinople," the Persian reported. "Tell me news of the Prince. Did he join us?"

Ahmed shook his head infinitesimally.

"Then now is the time. Now, it is safe."

Vlad's inky brows furrowed above his eyes.

Ahmed nodded to the unfamiliar man, then stood. As the door eked closed, he clapped, effectively interrupting Master Emine.

"The Sultan and his family have gone to secure an alliance with Hungary and her troublesome Christian leader, John Hunyadi, by way of Constantinople, perhaps. Or they may make Hunyadi and the lot of his countrymen slaves." Ahmed let his words hang there in the uneasy silence. "Either way, now we are free to conduct a special lesson. Come! You join us as well, Master Emine."

Ahmed swept out the door, his robe dancing behind him like a captive dancer. Vlad exchanged a look with his tutor, whose face had gone from desert brown to ashy with Ahmed's sudden display.

"I said come!" Ahmed's voice was thick with annoyance from the hallway. "And bring the blind boys!"

Several men in robes rushed in, curved daggers hanging precariously from their belts. One grabbed the whimpering Luca while another grabbed Andrei as he helplessly pawed the air. Each were yanked to their feet in tandem, to the tune of the robed men's laughter.

By way of a sideways glance, Vlad studied the blinded boys. Their eyes, no longer human in nature, were permanently swollen in odd places whilst gaping in others, all the while seeing nothing.

His thoughts flitted back to Saint Sabbas the Goth and imagined him smiling, cheerfully awaiting death, all for his Christian faith.

Luca and Andrei did not smile. They were not overflowing with courage and willingness to accept certain death, no matter how vile a form it may come to them. They were terrified in the darkness where he had put them when he chose to run away. The same darkness they would know forever during their time on earth. Their young faces, horrifically aged since coming to Tokat Castle, had fear etched into every plane, every crevasse, every feature.

*Perhaps I could borrow your courage, Saint Sabbas. If it were my torture and death, I could smile. But the torture of those loyal to me? No. That is a brand of cruelty that a man should not understand. Would you have been so hungry for death, had the lives of others been the ones at stake as opposed to yours?*

The hapless lot of Wallachian prisoners, flanked by one Turkish tutor, trailed Ahmed and his henchmen through the winding, candlelit halls. In all Vlad's years of captivity at Tokat Castle, he was certain that he had never traveled these particular halls before. The ceiling was lower and the grade, much steeper. They seemed to be going downhill, while the hallways to the dining room and the various bedrooms of the men all led uphill. Vlad kept his chin held high despite the trickle of fear that chilled the blood within his veins. He shivered.

"Fear not, Prince." Master Emine's voice was low, so that only Vlad could hear. "Fear not and hold on to the faith that defines you so well."

Vlad nodded to show acknowledgment, but the fear in his beloved tutor's voice shook his kind words. Master Emine shared a faith with Ahmed and the others, while Vlad shared a faith with an ever-dwindling number of captives. For his tutor to say such a thing made Vlad love him even more.

Finally, Ahmed slowed to a stop at a dark doorway. Luca's whimpers filled the tiny space. Or perhaps they belonged to Andrei. Nobody else dared make a sound.

"There are consequences for every action. Or inaction." Ahmed pushed open the heavy door. The musty smell of urine, feces, and rotted meat rushed over them in a hot burst of air. Someone retched, others groaned. Still, someone whimpered helplessly.

Vlad set his jaw, and his skin prickled as he realized at once where they were. Ahmed had brought them to the lion's den.

From the deep, dank, darkness, a beast growled. Some of the Wallachian boys began to whimper, and Vlad could hear Master Emine's quiet prayers come quicker and quicker still.

"I made a promise, that if Prince Vlad Drăculea refused to obey, Luca and Andrei would be thrown to the lions. Do you recall this promise of mine, Prince?"

Vlad nodded, though he was unsure if Ahmed could see him clearly in the darkness. "I do. But you shall not throw Luca and Andrei to the lions today—nor shall you ever."

Ahmed's eyes widened. Almost a full minute passed as Ahmed stared at him through the veil of dim darkness. Vlad, harnessing the courage of Saint Sabbas, stared back, unflinching. He clenched his teeth against Ahmed's impending anger, against the anger he had tried so hard not to elicit, against the anger that would come boiling out of Ahmed like lava from Mount Vesuvius. Vlad mentally steeled himself for the beating that he knew was coming.

Instead of contorting in rage, however, Ahmed's face cracked into a wide, wicked smile. His teeth, pointy and shiny white, seemed to glow in the darkness. And he laughed. Laughed until he doubled over and held his sides. A few of the robed Turks joined in, though their laughs were uneasy and awkward, nothing like Ahmed's.

As quickly as it began, Ahmed's insane laughter ceased.

From the darkness, a lion roar punctuated the disturbing scene.

"Prince Drăculea, you are right." Quick as the striking of a viper, Ahmed reached into the throng of them and grabbed Master Emine. His tutor's journal hit the ground and papers fluttered around them like birds, falling dead from a tree in winter.

Before Vlad could make any move to stop him, Master Emine was shoved through the food well, down the chute, and straight into the lion's den. His surprised shriek followed him, a moment too late, before he met his death.

The lion, now obviously joined by another, growled and roared to the tune of human screams and bone chilling shrieks.

"Blasphemy," Ahmed shouted, "will always be punishable by death."

*Master Emine blasphemed by telling me not to fear my captors and to hold on to my faith.*

Tears pooled in Vlad's eyes and trickled down his cheeks as the lions ripped his only friend to shreds.

## Capitol Nouă

Outside Târgovişte, Wallachia
in the Year of our Lord, 1447

*Put your sword back in its place, said Jesus, because all who live by the sword will die by the sword.*
~Matthew 26:52

"Do you not think it a bit odd, Father, to attend a dinner so impromptu as this?" Mircea tried to keep the worried tone out of his voice, but something was off tonight, and he had kept his mouth shut about it to his father long enough.

The great tapestries he had looked at every day for the whole of his life still hung in their places in the great hall. The long wooden table that sat before the members of the royal Drăculeşti household, where they had taken all their meals as Wallachian rulers for as long as he could remember, was unchanged. Even the area at the far end of the wooden table, where he learned to pull up and walk as a young boy, was no different than it had been any other day of his life. Everything about this castle was home, so what was it about this particular time that made everything about tonight seem so out of place?

Vlad II grinned but did not meet Mircea's gaze. Instead, he

sipped from his goblet of wine and stared out into the crowd. "Odd? My dear lad, what makes you choose such a word to describe this lovely evening?"

Mircea fingered his goblet of wine and tried not to seem too bewildered. "For starters, Father, we just received this invitation to a dinner, thrown in our honor, today. Yet when we host dinners, we send out the invitations weeks in advance, as is proper."

"Do they not seem as though they are prepared?" His father drummed his fingers on the wooden tabletop. "It would not do much good to throw a surprise dinner in our honor if they were to give us advance warning, now would it?"

"Yes, they seem very prepared. That is what is odd." Mircea sucked in a breath and let it out slowly. "Why would our nobles host a dinner for us and take care to construct a seating chart which sat our personal guards in an entirely separate section of the castle for the duration of the main meal?"

Mircea tried to remember an instance when this had been done before—any case of when this very thing had occurred in the past, but try as he might, he could recall none. His niggling feeling of unease refused to be quieted, despite the delicious smells that wafted in from the kitchen, which promised a delicious first course to this peculiar evening.

Mircea lifted his goblet to his lips, then set it down. "Father, I—"

The Voivode of Wallachia drained his goblet of wine and held it high above his head. It was refilled at once. "My boy," Vlad II slurred, "these are our boyars, our nobles. Do you not realize it is these very people who keep our Drăculești dynasty on the throne of Wallachia?"

Mircea studied the faces of the people. *His* people. "They all appear so . . ." He searched his vocabulary for just the right word. "Angry."

"*Pshaw.*" The older of the two waved his hand nonchalantly. "Stuff and nonsense. Relax and drink your wine. It really is deliciousable tonight."

"Deliciousable?" Mircea drummed his fingers on the ancient wooden table then, with a defeated sigh, picked up his goblet again and lifted it to his mouth. "Well, if it is good enough to coin a new word—"

Then, there it was. Something so infinitesimal that it should have gone unnoticed, and it almost did. The hint of a bitter smell that had no place in a cup of red wine. Mircea ran his finger around the rim, then rubbed his them together. Something was there. Powdery white and gritty.

*Poison.*

"Father!" Mircea leaned to whisper his concerns to the Voivode of Wallachia, but his seat was empty.

Mircea looked around. Vlad II was not speaking to a noble nor was he complimenting a guest. Instead, after only three goblets of wine, he was amid the boyars, dancing erratically to absent music with drunken movements.

Mircea's mouth hung agape as the harsh reality of their predicament sank in.

*Dear God, this has all been a setup. A ruse!*

Someone cued the music as the poisoned Voivode of Wallachia danced mindlessly in the midst of those who meant to assassinate him.

Mircea pushed back from the table, toppling his chair in the process. He clambered over the table, ignoring the sideways looks as he knocked into servants and nobles alike. "Father!"

A throng of people crushed in around their witless ruler.

"Father!" Mircea stopped trying to reach his father. It would have been impossible to do so at this moment, anyway. He cupped his hands around his mouth and yelled. "Father, this is a trap! A trap!"

The elder Vlad paid no mind and laughingly downed another goblet of wine that had been pressed into his hand. The crowd began to tighten around Mircea, suddenly unable to breathe, as he turned and shouldered his way through the people, away from his father.

*I must . . . I must escape!*

As he reached the door, he heard the heavy wooden beam fall across it from the outside. He pressed the door then pressed it harder. It refused to budge.

Behind him, the music cut suddenly, and everyone shushed. Everyone except the poisoned Voivode, who was laughing like a foolish simpleton.

The voice of Roman Snagov, the richest of the boyars, boomed into the sudden silence. "You have made a grave mistake in your secret alliance with the Ottoman Empire, Vlad Drăculea II."

His father's laughter slowly died down, and he glanced around, glassy eyed and grinning, at people who stared back at him with angry eyes. "In my, my what?"

"For your transgressions against your natural Christian ally, John Hunyadi of Hungary and Transylvania," Roman continued, "your punishment shall be death."

An excited chatter lit the crowd's murmurs.

Roman, however, was far from finished. "You allowed your sons to be slaughtered for the sake of Christendom, so you say in your own words, leaving only two more sons of the Drăculeşti dynasty. Mircea, your legitimate heir..." Roman glanced around for Mircea, but did not see him right away, so he continued.

"And your illegitimate bastard, Vlad the Monk."

Mircea backed through several people until his back hit the castle wall.

Roman's voice rose to a thunder. "You have single-handedly killed half of your sons without a thought!"

The boyars cheered Roman on.

"We will spare Vlad the Monk," Roman yelled, "since his mother is a boyar like us, on the condition that he denounces your name and your line." He looked around slowly. A few other boyars licked their lips, as though eager to taste what venomous words he spat at their Voivode next. "Now Vlad, thanks to your foolish transgressions, you have single-handedly brought an end to the reign of the Drăculeşti dynasty."

"Is this some sort of joke?" The helpless look as his father searched the faces of those whom he considered friends up to this very instant twisted Mircea's heart. "I have never transgressed against you, good people of Wallachia."

The back doors of the dining hall opened with a crash, and the royal guards filed in.

The worried creases on Vlad II's brow softened. "There now. My guards are back. This can all be sorted out."

"Guards!" Roman's voice was hard compared to the pleading one of the Vlad. "Kill the traitor."

*They are going to kill Father. Then, they are going to kill me. The Drăculești line will be no more.* Mircea turned away as the guards, men he had known since he was a boy, rushed his father, daggers drawn, with a blood-chilling battle cry. He turned and leapt at the door again. Still, it refused to budge. He glanced around to the hideous screeches of pain and death. A small window beside the door caught his eye.

Roman's voice boomed in the once-happy room that had transformed into a bloody battlefield. "Prince Mircea Drăculea is getting away! Stop him!"

All eyes in the castle dining hall turned to him.

Roman's voice was a roar. "Noblemen! Let Mircea Drăculea not live to see the sunrise!"

Mircea leapt and caught the window. As swords and daggers clanked beneath him, he pulled himself through the opening and landed safely on the other side. He did not pause in the cool night air to check his ankle which popped when he landed, but instead stumbled as fast as he could toward the darkness—and safety—of the Transylvanian Alps.

†††

Mircea stayed high in the gnarled, old tree in the marshland as the boyars searched for him. Their torches lit the Transylvanian countryside and curled like a flaming serpent beneath him, into ravines, and over hills.

*There are so many. All of the Wallachian nobles were in on this coup*

Still, nobody had come near his tree.

He breathed a sigh of relief and tried to let his aching muscles relax. His ankle throbbed, but he propped it on a branch and did his best to ignore it. Sleep tugged at his eyelids, and he shut them for a few seconds or perhaps a few minutes. *Perhaps, just perhaps, I can get out of this with my skin on.*

Moments, or possibly it was hours, later, a shrill bark met his ears. Cold, unfeeling laughter pricked his ears from somewhere in the darkness and forced him to wake with a start, heart pounding.

Mircea rubbed his eyes as the deadly realization set in.

*They have turned out the hounds.*

Tears eked down his once-royal cheeks.

"It is all over now, Prince," Roman called from the base of his tree to the tune of the bloodthirsty, barking dogs that were always kept hungry for such times as this.

On Roman's signal, two guards started up the tree after him. Shaking off the shroudy remnants of sleep, Mircea attempted to climb higher, though somewhere in his heart, he knew it was a useless maneuver.

The men, warm, fed, and rested, caught up to him easily. Mircea recognized their faces at once. *Johan and Igor.* Johan's wife died in childbirth last winter. The baby had been a girl, their first after a trio of boys. She had joined her mother in death shortly thereafter. Johan had named the baby after Elizabet, the Voivoda of Wallachia, Mircea's own mother.

Igor, overly tall for a Wallachian, sported green eyes and curly hair. When Mircea was but a small tot, Igor would sneak treats of sweets and toys into the nursery for him. His favorite had been a tiny, carved toy horse that rocked on rockers. He had carried it everywhere as a child and by the time he handed it down to Radu, most of the bright paint that had colored it so festively had rubbed away. Radu had not minded in the least. Despite the long connection with the two men, and all the years shared between them, the faces of both men were now blank. Expressionless. Neither friend nor foe.

They were the faces of men carrying out orders, men whose only true loyalty was to their stomachs and to their own families, stomachs that would go empty if an order was refused.

Mircea could not find it in himself to be angry at either Johan or Igor. Not even Roman, really. The true anger that burned in his soul was centered on one person and one person alone.

*Not only did you kill Vlad and Radu, Father, but you have also killed yourself. Now, you have killed me, too.*

The branch Mircea clung to so tightly cracked beneath his weight. In an instant, the broken branch sent a defeated Mircea tumbling past the two soldiers and into the throng of boyars and barking dogs—all of whom were thirsty for his blood.

†††

"Strip him naked," Roman ordered. "Then stake him out in the spread-eagle position." Roman buffed his fingernails on his lapel as several boyars rushed, swords clanging like church bells, to carry out his orders. He was in charge, and the feeling was intoxicating.

"Do you know what time it is?" A hunched old woman with crazy eyes and a kettle appeared at Roman's side.

He glanced at the moon and shook his head.

"It is time for tea." Something about the woman made him uneasy, but he shook off the feeling, lest it chase away his high.

"I did not expect to take the eldest Vlad so quickly," Roman confessed to the woman who appeared from seemingly nowhere. "Or so easily. The blasphemous old fool certainly did not put up any sort of fight, did he?"

The old woman's eyes sparkled with a wicked light. "When are we going to have tea?" She shook her kettle at him.

Roman ignored her. "The coup is over. I have earned my pay from the late Voivode's brother, Vladislav, for assassinating him per John Hunyadi's instructions." He stepped over to a quivering, naked Mircea and looked down at him. "Your father killed his two young sons, Vlad III and Radu. Their blood is as much on his hands as they are of the Ottoman devil, Sultan Murad and his son, the sometimes Sultan Mehmed, who actually killed them."

Mircea did not answer. His entire body shook, whether from terror, nakedness, positioning, or the cool of the night's air, he could not tell. Even though his lower lip trembled, the Drăculeşti heir made no sound.

Roman continued. "Your foolish father broke the sixth commandment the moment he traded them into the hands of the Ottomans. Do you remember your commandments, Prince?"

A tear rolled from Mircea's eye in answer. It tracked down his temple and ran into the expanse that separated his naked body from the ground. He fought to hold his head upright, as it was his arms and legs that were staked tight, not his head.

"Selfishness. Pure selfishness murdered those two young boys and countless others," Roman continued, "all so your pretender of a father could secure a peaceful reign for himself. Perhaps he is making his excuses to God as we speak before he is cast into the fiery pit of hell for all eternity."

Roman tapped his foot. "I am certain you are wondering about the fate of your elder half-brother, Vlad the Monk."

Mircea's head dipped backward.

"You will be satisfied to know that Vlad the Monk will be left to live, as he likes the late Voivode even less than we boyars do. Which brings me to you." He nudged Mircea's torso with the toe of his black hunting boot. "With your father taken so quickly, I have all the time in the world to get rid of the last of the Drăculeşti line."

The old woman shook her kettle again. "Then can we have some tea?"

"Certainly," Roman said, as he cast a glance at the old woman.

Something in her eyes made him glad she was not standing over his own nude, defenseless body. He shivered and looked away from her. His gaze fell at once to Mircea, whose helpless whimpers may well have been dog whimpers for all the attention he paid them. He was running on an exorbitant high, and his bloodlust was strong. But above all, he was in *control,* and the old truism had proven true. Revenge was a dish which did truly taste sweeter when served cold.

"Where should we start?" Roman stood over his bare, defenseless prisoner and thought but for a moment.

"Skin him alive!"

The boyars roared with excitement as his men, armed with knives and swords, rushed forward to relieve Mircea of chunks of his flesh. Roman's excitement for pain, torture, and death surged as Mircea found his voice somewhere between the slices and screamed for mercy. His pleas, however, fell upon Roman's heart that may well have been made of stone.

Before the momentum could fade, Roman pumped his fist into the air. "Start a fire beneath the prisoner!"

The old woman, grinning now and with a sadistic gleam in her eye, was all too eager to assume that task. "I knew it was time for tea."

As the boyars jammed wood beneath Mircea's bleeding body, she started the fire expertly beneath him. Once it had sparked to life, she thrust her kettle into the blazing fire. Mircea's screeches crescendoed into a howl as the flames bit into his oozing, freshly skinned body.

Roman watched with a sadistic glee as the pretender's son and heir roasted before him. He scratched the front of his pants, thoroughly pleased with himself for having constructed such an effective coup so quickly. His gaze fell upon Mircea's shriveled manhood, and he paused a moment. "Emasculate him!"

"No!" Mircea's already strained voice pleaded with a shrill shriek. Its echo off the mountains seemed to go on forever.

Drăculeşti blood dripped into the fire and sizzled as the ferocious boyars descended, yet again, onto the helpless Mircea. A sickly sweet smell hung heavy over the torture scene as they came at him again and again with flashing knives and slashing swords. When they were finished with their task, it was shocking that Mircea had any life left in him at all. His skin, torn off in haphazard chunks. His genitals, sliced off with reckless abandon.

Yet, when they allowed the hounds to gut him, Mircea's whimpers proved that he was still conscious. However, when the sour faced, smiling old woman came at him with the boiling kettle to fill his empty insides, his screams, delivered at an inhuman octave, brought a howl from the nearby wolves.

When dawn's early light breached the tips of the Transylvanian Alps and illuminated the hideous scene, the boyars, having grown tired of the torture, snoozed beneath nearby trees. Even the dogs, filled with Mircea's insides, slept. Roman, though, was nowhere near satiated. He stood over Mircea's charred and broiled body and spoke as freely as he ever had before. "As you can see, Prince, the Drăculești line can never suffer enough to please me."

A tiny moan issued forth from Mircea's lips.

"If only Vlad II, the former Voivode, had given me a position at court all those years ago, perhaps I would not have had to live in rural Wallachia. Had I not had to live in rural Wallachia, I would not have lost my only child to the band of marauding Ottomans that descended upon the Wallachian countryside like a biblical plague, under the cover of the night, to steal my precious son, Luca Snagov."

Mircea lapsed in and out of consciousness, but Roman did not care. These thoughts, these feelings, so strong within him for so many years, had been loosed. There was no reining them in now.

"If Luca had been spared, then my wife, the most beautiful girl in my childhood village, with her long black braids and her big, clear, green eyes—she would not have gone stark raving mad when Luca was wrested from her grasp by the torch-wielding Muslims. Had she not gone mad, she would not have snatched our family's sword from above our mantle and chased our son's captors, with only a few other hysterical and wailing mothers, as far as the law would allow, only to fail to save our son. And then, seeing no other way to live in this world without him, drown herself in the Danube."

Roman slowly drew his dagger from its sheath and tapped it against his side. "She knew what the Ottomans did to these young boys, you see. She could not live with that knowledge."

Mircea whimpered again, the life refusing to leave his body though he wished it would.

"Perhaps," Roman continued, "if Vlad II would have allowed me to raid into Ottoman territory, which I fell to my knees and so desperately begged for, in order to find the stolen Wallachian boys, perhaps he would still sit on the throne today, alongside you, Mircea." His palms grew sweaty, and he tapped the dagger faster. "Alas, he did not," Roman explained to his semi-conscious victim. "Instead, your father chose to side with the devil himself, the Sultan Murad and his devil son, Mehmed, who could not rule for more than two years before abdicating." Roman spat into the fire. "But most importantly, your father chose to do nothing at all to help my son."

Mircea moaned.

"He sacrificed not only his own children, but he sacrificed my child, too. And he smiled as he did it." Tears that Roman had thought long dry sprang to his eyes. "If only he had let me go and at least try to bring them home. All of this, all of it, would have been avoided. I would have made certain of it."

Mircea's eyes, half-glazed, seemed to focus on him for a moment.

Something nameless twisted in Roman's chest. "I could not risk you turning out like your imbecile father. I pray you understand— if you are capable of understanding anything besides greed and treachery."

Whatever almost human emotion that had twisted in his chest moments before transformed back into one that left him ravenous for more agony. The hurt from the years of living alone with only his hatred for the Drăculești family to keep him company, still boiled hot in his veins. Torturing Mircea and executing Vlad II, though necessary and profitable, had done nothing to quench his hate.

"Dig the pretender's grave," he shouted to the few remaining boyars who managed to keep their eyes open. "This is over. It is time I pay you all for your role in this coup."

When the hole was dug and his mangled body tossed inside, Mircea Drăculea was still breathing.

# Capitol Zece

Tokat Castle, Turkey
in the Year of our Lord, 1447

*Look upon my suffering and deliver me, for I have not forgotten Your Commandments.*
~Psalm 119:153

Two robed guards pulled Vlad, hard, toward the Sultan's chamber. Weeks had passed since Master Emine's murder, but Vlad's anger still pulsed in his veins. Ahmed led the way with his long strides that bespoke his trademark haughty arrogance.

"No!" Vlad yanked and writhed.

Ahmed stopped the procession, turned, and smacked Vlad across the face with the back of his hand. "Shut your fool mouth. The Sultan has summoned you for *other* matters."

With rough hands, the guards shoved Vlad through Sultan Murad's ornate, arched doors. He stumbled inside.

Sultan Murad, who resumed the throne after his son, Mehmed abdicated only last year, raised his sleepy eyes to Vlad, as he had so many times before. Despite being flanked by the guards and Ahmed, Vlad readied himself into a fighting stance.

"Welcome, Prince Vlad." Murad looked from Vlad to his wife, who sat nearby, covered in veils. All that was visible were her eyes, and they stared markedly at the ground. "Please, relax. Take a seat where you will be most comfortable."

Vlad did not have to look around to see the fine luxury that filled every nook of Sultan Murad's chambers. Overstuffed pillows. Gauzy veils draped here and there. Solid gold serving implements. A lute player playing from the corner. An oversized hookah. Platters of fruit, the likes of which Vlad had never seen before, and a pair of white tigers who lay sleeping beside the Sultan, secured with golden chains.

The chambers had belonged shortly to Murad's son, Mehmed II, when he reigned for two short years at the age of twelve, before abdicating in favor of his father. Rumors around Tokat were Mehmed felt as though he was not ready for such an undertaking. Vlad commiserated with the young Mehmed, who was his age. However, he felt he could have securely sat upon the throne of Wallachia at a much younger age.

*Perhaps if his father treated him the way he has treated us, he would have learned a thing or two about being a steadfast ruler*, Vlad thought darkly.

Vlad stared straight ahead and ignored the welcoming tone in Murad's words. "You are not touching me today. Not today, not ever. So it would be wise of you to not even try."

The Sultan yawned. "Prince Vlad, this is a *different* kind of meeting."

Vlad glanced at Ahmed, who patted his chest and smirked. *My letter from Ioana.*

The doors opened again and in filed Radu, his fine robes dripping with extravagant jewels. A throng of women followed him. Their eyes were downcast, like those of the Sultan's wife.

Vlad's jaw went slack. This was the first time he had seen Radu since his conversion to Islam. In addition to his luxurious wardrobe and fine foods, he had his own quarters at the Sultan's court—and his own harem.

*Judas*, Vlad thought. *You are a Judas.*

Without offering even a glance to Vlad, Radu strode past his older brother and kissed the Sultan in greeting before taking a seat intimately at his side.

"Now that you are both here, I have news from Wallachia which impacts you both."

Vlad, still standing, did not speak.

"Vlad Drăculea II, Voivode of Wallachia and friend to the Ottoman Empire, was assassinated. We received word that Wallachia is now in disarray."

"Did Mircea not assume the throne?" Vlad spoke freely, as though he and the Sultan were the only two in the room.

Ahmed's voice was a roar. "How dare you speak to the Blessed Sultan in such a defiant manner!" He drew back his arm as though he meant to knock some sense into Vlad.

The Sultan raised a finger. "Ahmed, to call me *blessed* makes you a blasphemer."

Blood drained from Ahmed's pinched face; his arm still frozen in the drawn-back position. "I do not understand, Ble—"

"Guards." The Sultan yawned again as though this drudgery was too mind-numbing to pursue any longer. "Seize the traitor."

The guards who had so roughly escorted Vlad did as they were ordered and grabbed a very surprised Ahmed instead.

"You killed my brother-in-law, Master Emine, while I was away."

Ahmed's mouth opened and closed on its own, but no sounds were produced.

The droopy eyed Sultan continued. "The punishment for blasphemy is death. Were those not your own words?"

Ahmed turned to Vlad. A seething hatred darkened his eyes. "You little liar. You spoke to the Sultan about me!"

"Silence!" the Sultan shouted. His white tigers, obviously unhappy to be awakened in such a rude manner, roared to punctuate the entire scene. "Prince Vlad said nothing of the sort. He is far more noble than thee!"

Ahmed sunk to his knees. Defeat contorted his normally haughty face into almost unrecognizable planes.

"Tell me truly, do you think that young Vlad is your only enemy in this court?"

Ahmed's head drooped.

The Sultan continued, unfazed by his unhappy, pacing lions. "Everyone in my castle answers to me. I know everything that goes on here. I need no subservient spies."

Sultan Murad rose to his feet. Everyone who was seated, except for his wife with the downcast eyes, followed suit. "Guards!"

They yanked Ahmed to his feet.

"Follow us with the blasphemer."

The Sultan nodded and extended his hands. "Prince Radu, Prince Vlad. Please, lead the way to the lion's den. I trust you now know the way, since you were privy to Master Emine's execution?"

"I was not present," Radu whispered. "I was with you, remember?"

"Ah yes, that is right." The Sultan giggled.

Vlad shuttered. *Rulers should never giggle.*

The Sultan continued, though he still gazed lustfully at Radu. "Prince Vlad, then. We shall follow you."

Without a look back, Vlad started toward the Sultan's door.

"Prince Vlad, wait."

Vlad turned. Nobody knew what the Sultan would command or what he would do. Vlad could just as easily swap places with Ahmed, and everyone in the room knew it.

The Sultan waved his hand. "Do take a torch. No use wandering in the dark like non-believers, is there?"

Vlad snatched a torch from beside the arched door and stared into Murad's dark eyes. "His words are a lamp unto our feet."

Nobody made a sound, until the Sultan laughed a strained laugh.

"Lead us then, Prince Vlad. With your *contemptuous* words."

The trek from the Sultan's room to the lion's den door proved to be a much shorter walk than it had been from his dungeon. Or perhaps the light from the torch helped more than he anticipated.

"Do place the torches in their sconces on the walls." The Sultan's command echoed off the damp rocks with an otherworldly quality.

Vlad and the guards did as they were instructed. Sure enough, the addition of torchlight brought a new dimension of hopelessness to this end-of-the-road torture ground. Miniscule bits of bones and teeth were scattered across the hard-packed floor, and odd shadows, trapped by the sudden light, jumped and twitched to find their way back to their deep, dark corners.

Vlad's eyes stopped on a scrap of paper stuck against the wall. *Master Emine. This is where Ahmed murdered you. Someday, my friend, I will avenge your death.* Beside the scrap of telling paper sat a small cage.

"Thank you for leading us, Prince Vlad." The Sultan joined Vlad at the mouth of the den. "Ahmed?"

Ahmed did not answer. Instead, he struggled against the guards' grips.

"Ahmed!" The Sultan clapped his hands together sharply. "Stop making a fool of yourself. Get into the cage."

"What?" Ahmed struggled and fought, but it was to no avail. "No!"

"Prince Vlad. Open the cage."

Incredulous, Vlad did as he was instructed.

"Guards, place the blasphemer into the cage. And lock it."

Radu stood in silence as the guards picked up Ahmed and crammed him into the too-small cage.

"Sultan," Radu whined with disgust. "The blasphemer urinated on himself. And on my foot."

Before they could slam shut the top of the iron box, Vlad cleared his throat. "Wait."

Silence befell the lot of them as Vlad strode over and yanked his letter from Ioana out of Ahmed's robe. Staring at the brutal man, he kissed the letter before placing it into his own robe.

Ahmed, his dark, wide eyes lit with terror, grasped wildly for his hand. He caught it, but Vlad jerked it away. "Vlad. Prince. Please. It was all in jest." He smiled wanly. "All of it."

"Why are you so scared of dying, Ahmed?" Vlad kept his face

stoic. "Do you not have a harem of virgins waiting for you in the afterlife, as you explained to me?"

Sultan Murad signaled his guards, who slammed shut the box and locked it. Then, he smacked the cage with his cane. "You urinated on my favourite! If I did not have cause to kill you before, I do now. Guards."

The Sultan stepped back and the guards opened the door to the lion's den. The same musty, rotten smell hit them at once. The fetid odor of urine and feces intermixed with rotten death made Vlad's stomach turn over. However, this time, nobody vomited. "The cage will ensure Ahmed is kept alive for the maximum amount of time and in the maximum amount of pain. No lion's paw can reach through the tiny openings, but their claws can."

Vlad watched, silent, as Ahmed's face transformed from scared to terrified from behind the bars. "No Sultan, please. Do not do this! I am but your faithful servant. Lowly am I."

The Sultan spat on the cage and whacked it again with his cane. "The lions will play with him before killing him. And dragging his body out in pieces to feast." A slow grin spread across the Sultan's face. "My lions do love a good game. And they are *very* hungry."

With a slight motion of his hand, the Sultan signaled the end to Ahmed's life. The guards plucked up the cage and dropped it down the feeding chute. The growls and roars from the lions almost drown out Ahmed's screams and pleas.

Almost.

"Shall we stay and listen?" The Sultan addressed Radu, who was still studying his dirty foot.

"No," Radu retorted, oblivious to the shrieks coming from the lion's den. "I would like to give my foot a bath as soon as possible. The blasphemer's urine stinks."

"As you wish." The Sultan motioned to Vlad. "Shall we return to my chambers to continue our talk?"

Vlad grabbed a torch from the wall sconce but said nothing. The Sultan's voice trailed him down the drear hallway.

"Oh, and guards? Stay there until the blasphemer is dead. No matter how many days it takes."

†††

Vlad entered the Sultan's room first but did not sit down. The Sultan and Radu followed him in and made themselves comfortable among Radu's harem and the Sultan's wife. Vlad could not help but notice it was now a different wife than before. The tigers stared at him and paced as far as their golden chains would allow.

The Sultan spoke first. "Now, where were we. Ah yes. Prince Vlad. You asked about your brother, Mircea, did you not?"

Vlad eyed the Sultan. He knew that the murder of Ahmed was orchestrated and perfectly timed just to draw him over to the Sultan's side. "I did."

"Your brother was tortured by the same Wallachian boyars that assassinated your father. Our men found him, buried alive, outside of Târgoviște. He did not live long after they pulled him out."

"Pulled him out?"

"Yes, of his hastily constructed grave."

"How did your Ottoman spies find him quick enough to pull him out, alive, if he was buried alive?" Vlad asked. Radu, however, seemed more interested in the Sultan, despite just having received the news of their father's and brother's deaths.

"Men, Prince Vlad. Not spies." The Sultan smiled. "And they found Prince Mircea because, when the boyars buried him, they left his head out of the grave."

Vlad tried to keep his emotions hidden. Inside, he was screaming. Anger boiled his blood and heated his veins until his hands shook, so he clasped them behind his back. He must have done well, because the Sultan continued.

"Your father was poisoned in a coup he never expected. Then killed in his own dining hall. By his own guards. Mircea though..."

The Sultan pulled up Radu's robes as one of his harem girls

brought a pan of water. He left his hand on Radu's thigh as the harem girl removed the soiled shoe and gently lowered his foot into the bath.

"Mircea was tortured for a long while. Expertly, it seemed. He was emasculated, roasted, and his guts were drawn from his body. Then, he was buried alive."

Vlad balked at the lack of emotion in the Sultan's delivery of this horrific news. The only emotion present in the room was the Sultan's lust for his baby brother.

*Why should he express emotion over death of his enemies?*

Finally, the pacing tigers sat down. "So, that brings me to the reason why I summoned you both here today. Prince Radu, Prince Vlad. Wallachia needs a ruler. And given the proximity and historic friendliness of Wallachia and the Ottoman Empire, I say they need a specially trained prince on the Wallachian throne. A person of *Turkish* choosing, so as to keep the historic peace between our two countries intact."

Vlad and Radu, still neither having looked at the other, remained silent.

The Sultan stood and spread his arms wide, kicking Radu's foot bath in the process. The harem girl yanked a veil from her midsection and began fervently dabbing at the water that splashed onto the floor. The Sultan paid her no mind.

"Which of you would like to go home to Wallachia?"

†††

Radu and Vlad both stared at the Sultan in silence. His pair of white tigers, obviously bored, roared again from the bounds of their golden chains.

"So," the Sultan asked again. "Who will it be? Who would like to be Voivode of Wallachia?"

Radu leaned across the bed and kissed the Sultan on the cheek. When the Sultan turned toward him, Radu continued to kiss him on the mouth, which the Sultan eagerly returned. Vlad, disgusted, looked away. His gaze drifted to the Sultan's wife, hugely pregnant and ever silent, as she simply ignored her husband's actions of affection toward another and continued to stare at the floor.

The Sultan's activities added to the long list of things Vlad did not understand about this country or this culture. The Sultan had many wives, while God's word clearly stated that marriage should be between one man and one woman, till death parted them. Only then could a man take another woman to wife, or a woman take another man as her husband. Radu, clearly not married, had a harem of women with whom he undoubtedly shared his bed.

*Adultery*, Vlad reasoned. *The same as adultery, he is being intimate with others before his wife.*

To see two men so blatantly affectionate with one another . . . Vlad's blood simmered as words from the book of Leviticus slapped themselves against the forefront of his brain. Not because of the actions themselves, but because Radu was not offended by these actions. He encouraged them. And worse, returned them.

The memory of the broken, homosexual men, led to the gallows by their father and brother before being hung like dogs flashed in Vlad's mind. The fact that his own flesh and blood condoned such unfathomable acts hurt even more.

The baby brother he tried to protect but could not. The baby brother who loved to cuddle, hated storms, loved the Wallachian palace animals, and cried when they got hurt or sick, loved their mother, and made up stories about fantastical creatures—all his innocence ripped away by the lusts of godless, heathen men without a shred of decency, without an ounce of compassion, without respect for human life other than taking it or ruling it.

"I do not know if I can bear to let you go," the Sultan whispered to Radu, his hand now on the inside of his thigh.

"Then let my brother go as I have no desire to go back to Wallachia." Radu's whisper was throaty and filled with lust.

"So be it." The Sultan motioned with his hand but kept his

attentions on Radu. "All hail Vlad Drăculea III, Voivode of Wallachia."

"Your Highness." The Sultan's personal escort appeared at Vlad's side. "Your things are packed, and the caravan is waiting. Shall we away?"

Vlad turned his back on the Sultan and Radu and motioned to a guard. "I will be taking Luca and Andrei with me. Collect them for me at once."

The Sultan laughed. "Did you dare give an order in the castle of the man who could strike you dead with a simple release of a latch from my tiger's chain?"

Vlad did not look back.

"I admire your fortitude, Vlad Drăculea III. However, your request will not be granted. Luca and Andrei, since they cannot serve in the Janissary Army as your late father promised, they will serve me as palace slaves, instead."

Vlad balled his fists. His first moments as a ruler and already, he was failing.

"How these things are done, Vlad III of Wallachia—" The Sultan's tone was mocking and arrogant. "You will go claim your rightful throne in your home country. Then, we can meet again in the future to negotiate payments and tributes. But as for today?"

He paused as though he was waiting for Vlad to turn around. Vlad did not.

Mehmed, who had appeared by his father's side without warning, interrupted. "Today, you are merely grateful to be leaving with your life."

Red tinged the outside of Vlad's vision. His palms were sweaty, and his fingers ached from being held in such a tight fist. Without speaking, he took two steps toward the door.

"Before you go take your rightful throne in Wallachia," the Sultan's voice was heavy. "Will you not you consider joining Radu and me? Just once?"

Vlad stopped walking but did not turn around.

"It would be interesting to compare the pair of you," Sultan Murad continued.

Vlad did not gratify the Sultan with an answer, nor did he turn back. Instead, he quickened his pace to the tune of their laughter.

"Prince Vlad?" The Sultan's sultry voice turned hard. "Do turn around. Now."

Vlad did as he was told.

Sultan Murad II stared hard at him. After a solid minute, he made a motion with his hand. One of his guards stepped from the shadows with a package wrapped in silk.

"A gift," the Sultan began, "for the new Voivode of Wallachia." He let his words hang in the thick air for a moment before continuing. "Compliments of the former Voivode of Wallachia, held in trust for you by your ally, the Ottoman Empire, for five years."

Vlad tried to hide the look of curiosity and appear stoic for the Sultan.

"What are you waiting for, Prince? Step forward and claim your prize." Mehmed laughed loudly until the whole of the court had joined in. He spoke through his chuckles. "It is not like it bites, Prince."

Vlad stepped toward the guard and with his chin held high flung back the silken cover. Before he could help himself, Vlad gasped. *My father's sword.*

He reached forward and grasped the ornate handle of the dragon-crested sword and hefted it high.

"In the hands of a true ruler," Murad gushed. "Welcome home, old boy."

Unable to find it within himself to thank the Sultan for anything, he simply nodded his appreciation toward him and stuck the sword, which had been a gift to his father from Pope Pious II when he was initiated into the Church's highly secretive Order of the Dragon, into his belt. He turned once again to go.

"Prince Vlad?" The Sultan's voice went flaccid again.

Vlad stopped advancing on the door. On his freedom.

"Perhaps I have something else you would want to take with you."

Vlad stopped and contemplated turning around. Before he could decide, someone slid a box across the floor. It bounced off his bare foot.

"Go ahead," Mehmed said. "There are no snakes in there." The sharp-nosed Mehmed laughed.

Vlad knelt and opened the box. Hundreds of letters, some yellowed and brittle around the edges, stared back at him. He picked through the top layer of letters. All boasted the same handwriting. Ioana. His Ioana.

Emotion knotted his throat.

"Ahmed had no access to them, I assure you." Sultan Murad's voice sounded almost human. "Or to her, at any time."

Something in Vlad cooled with the Sultan's reassurances, though he knew deep in his heart, that the man could not be trusted. He willed the emotion he was feeling not to show on his face as he picked up the box and tucked it under his arm. Without looking back towards the three Ottoman men who sat behind him, he continued once again toward the door.

"Wait." Hearing Radu's voice surprised him. Vlad turned around at once.

For the first time in almost five years, Vlad's eyes met Radu's. Something flickered across Radu's face, along with a quick, brotherly smile, before he pulled a golden rope. A curtain fell away from the wall, effectively revealing stacks of boxes, exactly like the one beneath his arm, which filled the space from the floor to the ceiling and lined the entirety of the Sultan's bedroom wall.

"Do take these, too," Radu said quietly.

"I wrote her a letter," Sultan Murad said, effectively breaking the familial connection, "and informed her you would be returning soon." He paused. "Judging by how well she keeps up correspondence, I am quite certain she will be more than a little happy to make your acquaintance when you resume your throne."

## Capitol Unsprezece

Tokat Castle, Turkey
in the Year of our Lord, 1447

*Brother will betray brother to death, and a father, his child.*
*~Matthew 10:21*

When Vlad was gone, and he and the Sultan had finished, Radu laid in the Sultan's arms. They had remembered to close the silk curtains around the Sultan's bed, an act they sometimes forgot to tend to, and the images of Radu's harem and the Sultan's wives moved about, just on the other side of them. The Sultan let his fingers dance down Radu's naked arm.

Radu shivered. "My brother never converted to Islam. He remains a non-believer. How can you trust him on the throne of his country when he could easily raise an army against you?"

The Sultan let his fingers trail from Radu's arm down his naked back. "My dear boy, you still have so much to learn. Your brother, Vlad III, will never, ever sit on the Wallachian throne."

Radu pushed himself up on the bed. He hoped he successfully masked the confused look from his face but was not certain he had been successful. "But my father and older brother were assassinated. Was that true or simply a ruse?"

The Sultan adjusted his large frame and made himself comfortable propped up on one elbow. The golden chains of the tigers rattled only inches away, secreted only by a flimsy curtain. "Yes, your father and brother, they are gone. In just the way I described. However, Wallachia already has a new ruler on its throne. Your uncle, Vladislav II."

"Vladislav? Of Wallachia?" Radu racked his brain. The only memories he had of the older Vladislav were bad ones, of coups gone awry and of leniency given too freely. He and Vlad had always referred to him as Dan. Not Vladislav.

"Of course. He assumed the throne after he had your father and brother assassinated by the boyars, on the orders of John Hunyadi of Hungary and Transylvania himself."

"A fact you neglected to share before." Radu bristled. "Sultan, you have sent Vlad into an ambush. Setting him up to be killed. For once he arrives in Wallachia to only find that Vladislav sits on the throne that he considers his . . ." Radu's thought trailed off. When he spoke again, his voice was charged. "There will be blood."

One of the women from Radu's harem peeked through the curtain, as did the Sultan's current wife in attendance. Murad waved them away dismissively. They disappeared at once. "Is that not a grand plan?"

"I personally do not see the grandiosity in it." A rough memory flashed in Radu's mind. It was hazy and held together with cobwebs but featured a great thunderstorm and a rocking chair. "Did you simply want Vlad killed?"

Murad shrugged. "His life brings nothing of substance or value to the world. As long as he remains a non-believer, he is better off dead. Best to be dead in darkness than live in darkness, I say."

The memory still plagued his mind. Other strands of the cobwebs reached somewhere, but he was not certain of the other aspects of the memory. *There was a quilt, perhaps?* Radu's brow knitted together above his eyes. "Why go through all of this trouble of making Vlad and I choose who would go?" Another thought burst into Radu's young mind. "And what would have happened to us, had I offered to go sit upon the throne of Wallachia?"

## Defender of the Faith

Sultan Murad shrugged. "What if you had? I tire easily of things. It will be amusing to see how it plays out, as it would have been had you gone in your brother's stead."

Radu's jaw went slack. *Am I that replaceable?* Before he could expound further on his thought, another string of the cobweb came into his mind. *It was Vlad. Holding me, wrapped in the quilt. Both of us rocking in the rocking chair as the storm raged on outside.*

Something twisted in Radu's chest, an emotion he could not quite name or place. Before he could say or do anything further, one of Murad's wives slid a platter of fruit through the curtain.

The Sultan plucked up an apple and continued. "Anyway, Vladislav is on the throne now, and alliances, as you are learning, are fleeting. Should the infidel Vladislav, or *Dan* as you so affectionately called him, not rule as we wish, we will simply have him assassinated." The Sultan bit into the apple, then offered it to Radu, who shook his head in declination. Something in the turn this afternoon took left him queasy and quite unsettled.

Once the Sultan chewed and swallowed the juicy bite of crunchy apple, he gave a belch, then continued. "The loyalty of the Wallachian boyars is all too easy to buy."

Radu swallowed hard. "And should Vlad decide to kill Vladislav and claim the throne as his own?"

"Then Wallachia will be his. However—" He took another bite of juicy apple and crunched it loudly before continuing. "Should Vlad decide to cross the Danube in any sort of hostile manner and therefore cross me, he *will* have the immortal life after death that those who follow Christ so desperately seek—and he shall live for millennia in *infamy*."

Radu pushed the odd sense of unsettlement to the back of his mind, giving room to puzzle over Murad's odd choice of words. "Immortal?"

"Those stupid, swayable Christians. The ones that he loves so much." Murad rolled his eyes and leaned back into the pillow. "Christians will not only fear his very name, but they will loathe him, should Vlad Drăculea III cross to me as anything less than a friend." The Sultan's eyes blackened, then cleared. "Or as a loyal subject."

Radu's face pressed into a mishmash of confused planes. The Sultan smiled and took another bite of the apple before offering it back to Radu. "They will think him the devil himself."

Radu accepted the apple, but only stared at Murad, who continued. "These Christians, what is the crux of their faith, Radu? Since you walked among them in your youth, what can you tell me about them? How they think?"

Radu thought back to the many Catholic Masses he had attended before coming to Ottoman captivity. He remembered the stone walls and the way the chants and hymns reverberated off those walls. He remembered the padded kneelers that folded down from beneath the pew in front of where they sat. He remembered the priest, who presided over the Mass in Latin. Without warning, the Communion hymn burst into his mind.

*Holy, Holy, Holy Lord God of hosts.*
*Heaven and earth are full of your glory.*
*Hosanna in the highest.*
*Blessed is he,*
*who comes in the name of the Lord.*
*Hosanna in the highest.*

"Well?" Murad's annoyed tone pulled him from his reverie. "Christians, they truly believe that they drink the blood and eat the body of their God, do they not?"

Radu slipped back into his rarely accessed memories. "Yes. They do."

*It is called the transfiguration. The highest point of the Mass, after the priest blessed the bread and the wine with a special prayer and the ringing of the bells that signaled the moment when the bread and wine truly became the body and the blood of Christ, so that the faithful could truly do as Jesus did with His disciples at the Last Supper on the night He was betrayed by Judas Iscariot.*

Before Radu could untangle the verses that swirled around all of his repressed memories that had come back to him in a flash, Murad continued. "On whose authority do they do this barbaric act?"

"On Jesus Christ's authority." Radu cleared his throat. He never talked about such things with the Sultan, because such things seemed to incite him to a killing anger more often than not. "In the *Mysterium fidei*."

"The Mystery of Faith," Murad translated. "How so?"

Radu began to recite. "At the time He was betrayed and entered willingly into His Passion, He took bread and, giving thanks, broke it, and gave it to His disciples, saying: take this, all of you, and eat of it, for this is my body, which will be given up for you." He dared a glance at Murad, who looked at him with wonder in his dark eyes, before he continued. "In a similar way, when supper was ended, He took the chalice and, once more giving thanks, He gave it to his disciples, saying: take this, all of you, and drink from it, for this is the chalice of My blood, the Blood of the new and eternal covenant, which will be poured out for you and for many for the forgiveness of sins." Radu sucked in a deep breath before finishing. "Do this in memory of Me."

Murad nodded. "I see. So, this belief is very engrained within the minds and hearts of the Christians, no?"

Radu nodded and tried not to let his uneasiness show as something icy slithered down his backbone at the memory of the faith he had forsaken.

*The unforgivable sin. Forsaking God's love for that of another.*

Beads of sweat cropped up on Radu's forehead, and he cleared his throat. "Yes. They do."

"So, we shall agree then. Vlad the Christian, will be a murderer. Murder breaks one of the Christian God's laws, does it not?"

"His Sixth Commandment," Radu whispered. "Thou shalt not kill."

"So kill he will," Murad continued, "and he will drink the blood of his victims before consuming their flesh. Vlad loves his Christ and his Saints to whom he prays, but should he cross me, he will forsake them all, for all eternity."

Radu was taken aback. "Forgive me, Sultan, but I want to make certain I understand."

Murad plucked the apple from Radu's fingers and commenced to chomping on on it again. He raised his eyebrows and signaled for Radu to continue.

"Sultan, if I understand correctly, what you are saying is that if Vlad does not behave in the way you have set for him, or if he should cross you at all during the entirety of his lifetime, you shall make known to all followers of Christ the world over that Vlad not only murders, but he drinks human blood and also eats human remains?"

Murad finished the apple and dropped the core onto the floor. A tiger paw fell atop it and pulled it from under the curtain. "You are entirely correct except for one aspect. Many people, unlucky people that they are, have not the education you and I have. They cannot read. So yes, I will tell Christians, and I will commission stories for those learned individuals to read for themselves. And for the rest, I have commissioned paintings in which Vlad Drăculea III, the one who has defied me against all odds, regardless of whether he reaches the throne of Wallachia or not, will forever forth be known as the bastard son of satan himself."

Radu stiffened. A wayward bead of sweat trickled down his forehead. Suddenly the room was stuffy. Much too stuffy. He coughed, then coughed again.

A harem girl slid back the silk curtains just enough to offer Radu a goblet of water, which he accepted.

"Would you like to see?"

After a long swill, Radu found his voice again. "Do you mean see the paintings?"

"Yes."

Before Radu could respond, Murad clapped his hands together sharply. The outline of his royal servants at once appeared, assembled with military precision, through the gauzy curtains. "Display the paintings!"

A sudden clamoring followed, then the world outside of the bed stilled. "Open the curtains!"

When the curtains were opened, two portraits sat before them.

As Radu gazed upon the first portrait, his scratchy throat, drier now than before, forced him to gag so much that he worried he may retch. Without being asked to do so, a harem girl at once refilled his goblet. Radu gulped the water greedily. "Sultan, did you commission Vlad to take the place of *Pontius Pilate...*"

"At the Crucifixion of Jesus Christ?"

Radu fought the urge to cross himself at the mention of the Crucifixion.

"You have a keen eye, Radu, among other positive traits," Murad praised, his lustful entendre heavy in his voice. "And yes, you are correct."

Radu stared at the horrific, graven image in dread.

Mehmed continued. "I commissioned this painting from an artist in Ljubljana. Of course, I shared with them a handful of stories about your ignorant brother for the artist's inspiration."

Radu's mouth fell open, and the goblet shook in his hand. "Ljubljana, north of Danube, in the land of Christendom."

"Some actually consider Ljubljana to be the most important region in Christian artwork." Murad stroked Radu's back. He shivered at his lover's touch. "So, tell me, Radu *cel Frumos*. What think you of this masterpiece of propaganda?"

Radu's mind raced. To speak truthfully and tell Murad that this entire, sickening portrait was blasphemous, to tell him that he hated each stroke of the brush that depicted Vlad III, who was once his brother, in such an obscene manner, to tell him that this portrait terrified him to the very core of his being, and that because of it, he wanted to run after Vlad, back home to Wallachia, to his mother, and beg forgiveness from both his brother and from God—these things would bring him disgrace, dishonor, and certain death.

And there was no possible way he could go back to the dungeon now. He would be viewed as a coward, as a traitor, among the Wallachians. They may even take retaliatory measures against him, what Wallachians were left, that is. And without his brother there to protect him— "The artist certainly captured the essence of the scene."

"Who all is depicted, oh newcomer to the truth?"

Radu gulped. "There is the Blessed Mother—"

"Ah," Mehmed interrupted, "you refer to *Maryam binat Imran*, do you not?"

Radu cleared his throat but did not answer. He refused to refer to the Mother of God by any name less befitting her glorious station, no matter what faith he called his. Instead of answering and subsequently angering Murad, he continued. "There is Satan, lurking about. Along with Saints Peter and John, and—the Sanhedrin?" *The Sanhedrin wearing a Wallachian royal crown?*

"Very good. Do continue."

"And the Roman guards. The Centurions." Radu's voice quieted. "And there, wearing the crown of the Wallachian Voivode, and in place of Pontius Pilate, is Vlad III, sitting in judgement of Jesus Christ." Again, Radu had to fight the urge to cross himself, an urge which he thought would be gone with his acceptance of Islam. He shivered despite the stuffiness of the room. He wished he could climb out of his skin, if he could, he would—

"I see you are well studied in the heathen iconography of the non-believers, though I would expect nothing less, given your upbringing." Murad scratched his nose as though he was speaking of menial things, things of no more consequence than asking for a ball of melon or fresh goblet of wine.

"How about this one here," the Sultan asked, "what do you make of it?"

Radu gulped, but the knot that had formed with the unveiling of the damning portraits refused to be dislodged. "Vlad III finds himself present at the crucifixion of Saint Andrew, some thirty years after the Crucifixion of Jesus Christ in 33 A.D."

*In nomine Patris, et Filii, Et Spiritus Sancti.*

A rabid flush lit Radu's neck and his words came out most incredulous. "You made my brother present at the martyrdom of Saint Andrew, the patron Saint of *Romania*?"

Murad shrugged. "Of course. It is most fitting, is it not?"

Radu swallowed hard. "By the same painter, as well?"

The Sultan scoffed. "My dear boy, of course not. This painter was *Russian*. And he does have quite the knack for painting the macabre, would you agree? His portrait of John the Baptist's head on a platter? Well, that one bothered even the likes of me."

Radu's stomach turned over. "And you shared with the Russian painter equally horrific stories of Vlad, I assume?"

"Different stories, perhaps a bit exaggerated here and there, but all in all, yes. Of course."

"I suppose tales of his most horrific nature will spread over the whole of Christendom by the time death comes for him, be it now or later."

"And after. You see, some paintings I have commissioned, they are not to be painted until several hundred years into the future. Such as an altar piece from Germany, also depicting Vlad at the *Crucifixion*, as you say, but playing a much less lethal role." Murad leaned back onto a pillow and scratched his exposed manhood.

Radu's heart thundered in his chest. "With a few strokes of a commissioned brush," he drew in a shuddering breath, "you have made my brother the enemy of the entire Christian faith?"

"You see Radu, even *Christians* have a price. I believe Judas Iscariot's price was a meager thirty pieces of silver, was it not?" Murad motioned for the paintings to be taken away. "The Christians he loves so mightily, like Luca and Andrei and all the ones he vies to protect, will turn on him, should these paintings ever be revealed."

A flood of mixed emotions wracked Radu's brain. Despite everything, Vlad had never purposefully done anything to hurt him, no matter how many times the Ottomans' whispered otherwise. And the fact that Murad had these paintings commissioned before Vlad was set to sit on the throne of Wallachia, it was as though Murad, the man with whom he shared not only his meals and his time, but also his body and his bed, had been planning Vlad's ultimate demise for quite some time.

Radu stuck his finger in his ear, a bad habit he picked up as a child and had never fully broken. Since coming to Tokat, some of his memories changed after listening to the Turks talk, but if he sat and thought hard enough, alone and in the quiet, he could pick out the truth. Still, sleeping in a bed was better than sleeping on the rocky floor of the dungeon, especially after enduring a beating—or worse. Since he consented to be a lover of the Sultan, life had become much more bearable. Radu shifted his weight and wiggled the finger in his ear to scratch an imaginary itch. Yes, there was no doubt about it, he had done the right thing to preserve not only his health, but also his sanity.

*Then why are your hands sweaty? Why do you fear that you have turned your back on the one who shares your blood? And the One who shed His blood for you?*

Radu shook his head again. Normally it was easy to quiet the incessant little voice that sounded strangely like that of his mother. It spoke to him less and less since he left the faith of his childhood, but today, it was loud. *Like the bells at the high point of Mass.* He cleared his throat to help drown it out.

Murad continued; his voice even quieter than the one in his mind. "Commoners will think Vlad III to be a Judas. Or better still, they will think him an immortal *beast*, not bound by the constraints of time, since as you so keenly saw, he is clearly present at events many, many years apart. Many, many years in the past. So perhaps those ignorant enough to believe in such superstition will welcome the idea of a time-traveling monster who looks like Drăculea, a fanged creature who, of course, drinks the blood of his victims with reckless abandon." Murad smiled a wicked smile and let his hand meander under the sheets until it met Radu's naked flesh.

Radu did not respond, nor did his body. He felt as though his head may well spin right off.

Murad continued darkly. "Yes, they will, those ignorant peasants. Rest assured that Voivode Vlad Drăculea III—should he succeed and claim his throne in Wallachia—will not dare cross me."

When Murad finished speaking, he pulled Radu back down onto the pillows. He did not bother to order the curtains be closed, nor did he pay any mind to their women standing only inches away from the pair of them. The only thing that crossed Murad's mind, besides plotting and exacting revenge, no matter how premature that revenge might be, was something he did to satiate his own personal satisfaction. Sometimes, that satisfaction was best filled with the bodies of men, other times, boys. Other times still, one of his many willing wives. That particular day, revenge was the course that whetted his appetite for satisfaction. For now, however, that satisfaction just so happened to be in the form of Radu Drăculea, now known as Radu the Beautiful.

# Capitol Doisprezece

## Wallachia
### in the Year of our Lord, 1447

*Truly I tell you, Jesus continued, no prophet is welcome in his hometown.*

*~Luke 4:24*

"There it is. That is the Danube!" Vlad heard the rushing river before it came into view and it was all he could do to restrain himself from spurring his gifted Ottoman horse on and racing for the boundary river. It just was one of the many things that he had dared to dream of during his five years in captivity.

The small band of sleepy Turkish forces that the Sultan had dispatched to escort Vlad, the new Voivode of Wallachia, across the Ottoman Empire and back to the safety of his own lands, sounded as thankful in their guttural sighs and grumbles as Vlad felt. Relief at being finished with their chore was more than evident by their broken Romanian words.

"This is as far as we are permitted to go," one said.

Vlad found this guard's voice to be cheerier in this one statement than any of the handful he had spoken since leaving Tokat Castle.

"Praise Allah," another chimed in, under his breath.

Vlad ignored them. Something twisted in his chest as he stood on Ottoman soil and looked across the all-important boundary river into his homeland—the homeland that, at times, he was certain he would never see again. Yet here he was.

Here.

*Home!*

He had made it and he did not have to run away in order to get here, nor did he have to come back in a coffin. No. He was here, so close and yet still so far. A rogue memory of Ioana wafted into his mind. As quickly as she appeared, he pushed her away.

*Not yet. Not until I am on Wallachian soil am I going to allow myself to dream of you. Whilst I am on the soil of the Ottoman Empire, I fear your memory would somehow be soiled by all that they did to me, all that they took from me. All that they are. I pray you wait just a little longer.*

With Ioana stowed safely back in the recesses of his mind, he was momentarily freed to think of other things. Vlad crossed himself and spoke to God. "Thank you for bringing me here, Father, though I never counted on seeing Wallachia again without Radu at my side. Also, without my father, wretch that he was, and Mircea here to meet me. However, life never really has taken the expected turns that I so counted on. I know, though, Your way is best." He crossed himself again. "*Amin.*"

Vlad opened his eyes and took in the sight laid out before him. Steep hills, solid, welcoming, green rose from out of the river's waters that reflected oh so perfectly the blue of the sky. He paused his thoughts for a moment in reverence.

*Home.*

The words from Deuteronomy spread out all around him. *The Lord, your God, who goes before you will fight for you, just as you saw Him do for you in Egypt.*

One of the guards interrupted his musing. "Do you still require our presence, Voivode Drăculea?"

Vlad, contented never to speak to an Ottoman again, simply shook his head.

"You will now make your way to Târgovişte. Alone. Goodbye, Vlad Drăculea III, Voivode of Wallachia." The Turk turned to go but stopped short. "Truly, I pray we do not meet again."

†††

Memories from his life before, before he was made a prisoner of the Ottoman Empire, before his faith was tested in unimaginable ways, before he lost his father and the two brothers he knew and loved so deeply, lurked behind every tree and within every shadow on his journey across Wallachia to the capitol city of Târgovişte.

For a few moments here and there, Vlad felt like a boy again. The memories of playing hide and seek in the Wallachian countryside with other boys who called the castle home were fresh. So fresh that he almost caught a glimpse of his former self now and again, darting behind trees and bushes, laughter all around.

Always near to him, was Radu. As the flitting memories played out around him, Radu's image winked out, like the nighttime stars that sometimes shone so brightly, while other times flashed and disappeared into blackness.

*Radu. God be with you.*

Before he could continue the prayer, Luca's contorted face flashed in his mind.

"Radu made the choice to live a comfortable life, in a Turkish Sodom and Gomorrah." Vlad's voice was a growl in his throat. "Luca was tortured, as was Andrei, simply for being loyal to Wallachia. And to me."

Regret burned hot in the back of Vlad's throat as he rode through the familiar woods. *You should not have left without them. Without Luca. You promised him that you would not leave him, and he no doubt still clings to that promise right now. God above only knows what the Ottoman devils have said about my abrupt departure, and their remaining there. Abandoned.*

If, nestled within the jutting spires of mountains, Târgovişte

DEFENDER OF THE FAITH

had not come into sight, Vlad may have turned his pony's face and headed straight back to Tokat.

But there, around his beloved castle, was something he could not place. Something bad.

He rode further ahead, but at a slower clip than before. The grumblings of soldiers in a musical language that were definitely not Romanian met his ear. He dismounted quietly and walked his Turkish horse quietly through the understory. A stream that was never anything more than a dry creek bed except during the rainy season, flowed freely now and tinkled along the rocks.

"We must have had rain today," Vlad mused in a voice that was little more than a whisper. He sat, still as he could and stared through the trees. "If I can catch a glimpse, just a glimpse, perhaps I can see who is there. And if they are friend or foe."

Minutes turned to hours as Vlad sat in the Wallachian undergrowth, listening to the strange language as it bounced down the flowing water. Since it only met his ears in bits and pieces, the linguistics proved themselves harder to place than if they had strung themselves along properly.

Lovely Ioana briefly invaded his thoughts, though her Romanian accent was thickly laced with a Grecian overlay. On the heels of her fleeting memory rode that of her father, John Hunyadi. His was a strong Romanian accent that sounded nothing like what the waters carried back to him.

Finally, a recognizable phrase with a certain lilt made him almost snap his fingers together in excitement. "Hungarian. They are speaking Hungarian."

The voices grew fainter. "Those are not my forces, nor are they Ottoman forces," Vlad said aloud. But nobody was there to hear. "Why would Hungarian patrols be outside my castle?"

An out-of-place sound came from the underwood which was backlit by the setting sun. Branches swayed and twigs snapped, but Vlad saw nobody.

Slowly, he drew his dragon-crested blade, the one that had been a gift for his father from Pope Pius II, from its sheath. "Who's there?"

"Those are your Uncle Vladislav's forces," a ratchety voice answered. Vlad watched as an old woman with only a few stumpy teeth and a crinkled smile appeared at the tree line. A green Gypsy *diklo* was knotted atop her head, and an assortment of jewels dotted every gnarled finger. "No need to fear, rightful Voivode of Wallachia. You will find only friends here in your forest." She held back an armful of tree branches. "Unlike the enemies that you will find at your court presently. Come into our camp. You are far safer with us tonight."

†††

"Welcome back to what is already yours, Vlad Drăculea III." A tall, skinny man with patchwork pants took his horse's reins and motioned to an overturned bucket next to the fire. "Please, sit with us. We have been waiting for you."

Vlad accepted the seat. "Waiting for me?"

"Yes." The skinny man offered Vlad a drink, which he readily accepted. "I am Tamas, your loyal subject. As are we all." He gestured to the whole of the Gypsy camp. "It was my mother, Mariela, who saw you coming."

The old woman with the crinkled grin beamed from across the fire. "Like a dragon, coming forth from the mouth of hell to save his people. Like Jesus will come, when He steps down from Heaven to save us all."

Vlad's eyes widened as Mariela produced a crystal ball from under a swatch of purple velvet. "You know what the godless heathens told you. About what happened to your father and brother. Now, would you like to see the truth?"

Vlad glanced down at the crystal ball that sparkled in the firelight. "I am a Catholic, Mariela. Looking into such things as this, in such a manner, is sorcery." He paused. "I appreciate your kindness very much. But I cannot look into your bewitched crystal."

Mariela did the Sign of the Cross with her free hand. "We too are Catholic. Do not doubt your God. He gave you the gift of endurance and the heart of a warrior." She did a motion with her hand so quickly that Vlad could not follow it. An ornate rosary appeared in her hand where moments before had been nothing at all. "This is from the Holy Land."

Enchanted, Vlad stood and walked around the fire to examine the rosary.

Mariela answered Vlad's questions before he could ask them. "The Hail Mary beads, carved from the branches of olive trees. The Our Father beads, from smoothed rosewood branches."

"And the crucifix?" Vlad ran his thumb over the smooth, multi-hued stone cross on which hung a silver corpus of Our Savior.

"Opal."

"Opal, I see." Vlad gave the rosary back to Mariela carefully. It was truly spectacular. "I have not seen its equal."

Mariela looked old and wise in the firelight. "God gave you those gifts, my long-awaited ruler. But not me. I have not the heart of a warrior, and my old body can only endure so much. He gave me, instead, the gift of sight." She gestured into her round-topped caravan. "See for yourself."

Feeling as though he was peeking into one of his father's court meetings, Vlad carefully peeled back a gauzy curtain and gasped. A glittering altar, featuring statues of the Holy Family that looked to be from the time of Jesus himself, stood between candles of differing heights. Ever reverent, Vlad genuflected and crossed himself.

"Without looking to the past, Vlad, there is no way to step confidently into the future." Mariela's voice came from behind him. "We have been waiting here for you. We hold the knowledge of the truth in our midst. It is time you see it for yourself."

*Mother Mary, please let these people be a gift from You and from Your Son, and not a trick from the evil one.*

Vlad followed Mariela back to the fireside where the crystal ball sat, waiting, on its purple fabric. "There are others that God gifted with the blessing of sight, you know."

Vlad looked thoughtful. "I have not heard of one."

"There are many." Mariela crossed her arms. "A young Franciscan Catholic, Colette. From France. She was a nun who will be a Saint. She foretold many prophecies."

"What did she foretell?"

"She was most famous for knowing the exact date and time of her own death."

Vlad nodded. "To know the time of one's death would be helpful for men such as myself."

Mariela's slight movements made the golden coins on her headscarf jingle musically in the falling darkness. "Saint Colette once delivered a baby who was stillborn. She wrapped the child in a veil that had been given to her by the Pope. She then handed the lifeless body to the father of the child and instructed him to take the child to the village priest, many miles away. The father did as he was told. By the time he reached the priest, the child was crying. Very much alive."

Gentle, knowing laughter sounded from the Gypsies seated around the fire.

"Saint Collette sounds like a spectacular Christian woman," Vlad agreed. "You said there were more? Seers, I mean?"

Mariela smiled. Her wrinkled face reminded him of his grandmother, in the firelight. "Of course. Saint Frances of Rome foretold the death of her daughter, Agnes. Also, her dead son appeared to her, along with the archangel God sent to watch over her." Mariela looked thoughtful. "Many of these blessed ones have seen Purgatory. And hell, as well."

Vlad tried to keep the sour note from his voice. "There are many kinds of gifts God gives his faithful followers. Aside from simply seeing."

"Simply seeing," Mariela scoffed. "There is nothing simple about this gift. Sometimes, I wonder why God blessed me with it, other times I wish I did not have it at all."

"Others have had this gift, too, you say?"

Mariela nodded.

"Tell me some more."

"As you wish." She closed her eyes and thought a moment. "The good Catholic Blessed Anna Taigi. She was gifted with foresight through a glowing orb that only she could see."

Vlad derided before he could help himself.

Mariela ignored him and continued. "Then, we have Saint Padre Pio of Pietrelcina, who was blessed with the stigmata."

*Ah yes. Wounds of Christ.* "I have not heard of Saint Padre Pio?"

"Of course not. Has has not been born yet."

Vlad's jaw went slack.

Mariela continued. "He will lead people to God through the Sacrament of Confession. And he will even hear the confession of the devil himself."

"Sultan Mehmed?" The satirical joke flew off Vlad's tongue before he could stop it.

"No, Satan."

Vlad stilled himself and tried not to think about Mehmed II in a confessional, though the thought of the actual prince of darkness setting foot in a confessional was a disturbing one. The very thought made his stomach turn over on itself.

Mariela ticked off her fingers against her thumb. "The illiterate French peasant girl, Saint Joan of Arc will make quite a name for herself as she leads people to God through her gift of sight. She will stand on God's Word, even though she cannot read it herself, and lead the French armies to victory against the robust English. This will be England's first time to meet defeat on a battlefield in over three centuries."

Vlad sat, silent.

"Saint Benedict of Nursia," she continued, eyes still closed. "Whose prayers delivered him time and again from the evil one's onslaught against him. Saint Martin de Porres, who struck a deal with the rats he was tasked to poison, and Saint John Masias, who saved a million souls from Purgatory—each of which came to battle at his deathbed as the evil one tried to ensnare him at the last possible moment, as we know he will."

*Pray for us sinners. Now and at the hour of our death, amin.*

"Saint Joseph of Cupertino, the flying friar—"

"Wait, flying?"

"Oh yes. When he would pray, he would levitate."

Vlad pursed his lips and narrowed his eyes.

Mariela continued. "He took a long time to come to God, but when he did, God gave him this gift. Joseph would have to chain himself to the floor, on occasion, to keep from floating away."

At this, Vlad could not contain his laughter. Hilarity he had not experienced in years roiled up from within him and escaped in long, hiccupping gasps. He gripped his sides and laughed until both Tamas and his mother Mariela were laughing with him, to the tune of the rest of the Gypsy camp's jovial giggles. After many moments, Vlad wiped the tears from his eyes and relaxed his shoulders.

"I have never heard of the likes of some of these people, these Saints, Mariela."

"That is because some have not had their time on earth yet. But they will."

Vlad nodded. "I believe you." Still, he hesitated.

Mariela's black eyes glistened. "You still fear we here do the devil's work."

*It is as if she is reading my mind.*

"Yes. Yes, I do."

"Truly I tell you, gifts from God are sometimes too majestic for our human minds to comprehend. When a gift from God is given, nothing is asked in return. Just as I ask nothing in return for helping you see the truth."

Vlad sat, stoic, on his overturned bucket as the night sounds of Wallachia's forest began to come to life around them.

"I do not ask for money. Or recognition. Or a place within your palace." Her wrinkled face softened. "All I ask is that you see the truth as I have been sent to show you. Because, dear boy, you have lived among the liars for far too long."

Moisture welled in Vlad's eyes. *She reminds me so much of Grandmother.*

"The occult is just as real as God," Mariela continued, "and you know this, having lived among the enemy." Her eyes turned flinty. "When a trick is issued from the evil one, there is always something that must be exacted. A price. A bargain. Nothing is given freely, but instead, *everything* is a trick. And the deal or bargain must be struck beforehand and agreed upon." Her voice deepened as though she had personal stake in this entire situation. "But the trickster is sly. What you agree upon is *never* what he intends to give. Or take."

Sultan Mehmed's sharp-nosed face flashed in his mind. *The evil one.*

The moon came out from behind a cloud and Mariela's eyes cleared. "I assure you, my Voivode, we seek only to do God's will. We are His messengers, here to assist you in regaining your rightful throne." She paused. "As a true Defender of the Faith, do you accept this gift from God?"

Vlad nodded. "I do."

Mariela sank into the dirt across from him. "Tell me the truth as you know it."

"Sultan Murad II told my brother, Radu that—"

"God save his soul," Tamas muttered. People who now filled the Gypsy camp crossed themselves and mumbled a quiet Romanian prayer at the mention of Radu's soul.

"We saw Radu commit the unforgivable sin." Tamas's voice sounded as though he felt he should explain. "A son of Wallachia. Forsaking the one true God for that of another."

"You saw this?" Vlad's blood turned icy in his veins.

"My mother saw everything. That is how we knew to camp here to wait for you."

"I see. You asked for the truth as I know it." Vlad shook off the uneasiness and continued. "The Sultan said the boyars killed my father and tortured my brother Mircea before burying him alive, which his Ottoman spies discovered. And they needed someone with Ottoman sympathies to place on the throne of Wallachia. It was between Radu and myself. I was chosen to come and quite thankful, truth be told, to do so."

"Have you Ottoman sympathies?"

Vlad shook his head. "No. I do not."

"Do they know that you despise them and all that they are, all that they do?"

"Yes, they know it. And they have known it every day that I was their prisoner, all five years' worth."

Mariela's earrings, long and multi-hued, clinked together like a windchime. She smiled. "Did you then think it odd that they chose to send you?"

Vlad shrugged. "I suppose. I fought them tooth and nail the entire time—"

"We know." Tamas smiled "We saw."

The tiny nighttime noises magnified around them. "Then yes, I was so eager to leave, I did not think about it too much. I suppose it does seem odd that they sent me instead of Radu."

"Now," Mariela crooned, "Would you like to see the truth as God, Creator of Heaven and Earth, wills it?"

"I would." Vlad bent over the crystal ball, and all the noises of the forest fell silent. He squinted into the orb and waited.

*In Jesus' name, God help me to understand the truth . . .*

Water from the bottom of crystal began to stir in time with his pounding heart. It sloshed from side to side, like the sea beneath a storm, until it rose up into waves. Heart thundering in his chest, Vlad watched as the waves splashed from both sides of the crystal, as though he was staring into the sea itself. White-capped waves splashed so hard, he feared it would shatter the crystal and all the water that had no business being in a crystal in the first place would come splashing out onto the Wallachian ground.

Before he had the chance to wrap his mind around why water

was sloshing around inside a Gypsy's crystal ball, forms began to take shape over the water. Vlad's heart pounded in his chest like a stallion, and his breathing came faster and faster still. He closed his eyes.

*This is it. The time is now.*

When he opened his eyes, the water had cleared from inside the crystal. What was left was something so incredibly familiar, he wanted to cry. Vlad's voice was incredulous. "It is Wallachia!"

And Wallachia it was. His childhood castle in the rolling Wallachian hills, under a starlit night. An entire world—*his* world—locked within the walls of the crystal ball.

Vlad watched helplessly as his father penned the infamous letter to the Hungarian king, John Hunyadi. He saw Mircea there, over their father's shoulder, and the look of horror on his face as the letter came to a bloody end. The painful words were brutally clear.

*Rest assured that I have broken peace with the Ottoman Empire since resuming my rightful throne by dealing with Christian kingdoms such as yours in a friendly manner and, in doing so, have betrayed two innocent souls. Vlad III and Radu Drăculea.*

*Please understand that I have allowed my children to be butchered for the sake of Christian peace, in order that both I and my country might continue to be vassals of the Holy Roman Emperor.*

Vlad watched as an unexpected enemy, Vladislav II, snuck up from nowhere and, with the help of John Hunyadi, laid claim to the throne of Wallachia. Then he watched as that same enemy, his uncle Vladislav II, handed satchels of gold to Roman Snagov, the grinning boyar with a bloodthirsty heart.

Vlad's breath hitched in his throat. *With the help of John Hunyadi, Ioana's father, my uncle paid off the boyars to assassinate my father and Mircea.*

"Vladislav," Mariela whispered. "He is as evil and blackhearted as any Ottoman."

"And it is Vladislav II, my father's own brother, who sits on my rightful throne this very night." Vlad's voice sounded foreign and strange. Almost otherworldly, like when his dreams refused to let him fully wake or fully sleep, but instead kept him locked in a nightmare world where nothing made sense.

Vlad blinked back the surprise at the change in his voice and looked back down into the ball. The macabre coup had been meticulously laid out in the form of an honorary dinner, and the happenings that led up to his father's and brother's deaths played out in rapid succession. Roman accepting the bag of poison from John Hunyadi himself.

"The root of belladonna," Vlad whispered to himself. "Deadly. Even if the guards had failed to take Father, he would still be dead."

The image in the ball cut to Roman as he dusted both Mircea and Vlad II's goblets with the deadly powder before they were filled with wine, as the intended victims sat at the royal table, completely unaware of what was about to transpire.

His father's gluttony, as he consumed glass after glass.

Mircea's hesitancy. *Always his hesitancy, never did he stand up enough to our father to make a difference. Now he paid for that with his life.*

The giddiness as the poison took hold of his father's faculties.

The betrayal and fear in his father's eyes as his very own royal guards rushed him on another man's command.

The entirety of the make-believe party was like a spear through Vlad's heart as he watched his father's bloody demise.

The image in the ball switched from the bloody murder of his father over to Mircea as he leapt in fear from the dining hall window, and ran from certain, unavoidable death.

More fear, almost tangible, as he climbed the tree and prayed.

The tense panic as he dozed. And waited.

Watching and feeling the terror, regret, and anguish that consumed Mircea as Roman and the traitorous boyars tortured him almost to death, before burying him alive but in unimaginable agony, was even more painful than watching the death of his father.

The image flickered yet again. The faces of Roman and the

boyars replaced the horrific images of the bloody coup that left him fatherless and brotherless. Images of laughing Roman, breaking bread with the same murderous boyars who killed his family now filled the crystal, and they dined in *his* rightful castle this very night. Vladislav's face was there, along with John Hunyadi, overshadowing all, like a black storm cloud just over the horizon.

Vlad glanced up at Mariela. "But where is the Ottoman Empire in all this?"

Almost before he was finished speaking, the image changed yet again. This time, it featured Radu and Sultan Murad conversing in the bedchamber as he himself was escorted from Tokat Castle. Their conversations played out before him, along with the damning portraits, and his suspicions were confirmed at once.

Vlad sat back, defeated. "I have no other blood in this world, aside from Vlad the Monk, the illegitimate brother who hates me perhaps as much as the Ottomans do."

From the corner of his eye, Vlad noticed the crystal clouding over. He sat forward and studied what was there. Beneath the fog, a figure began to take shape. His breath hitched in his throat. "It is. . ." He leaned closer still. "Ioana."

Her raven hair, unbound, flowed over her shoulder. It blew gently in the nighttime breeze as she stood on a castle's balcony. Still as beautiful as ever before, her ivory skin did not glow as it had when they were children, and her angelic smile was downturned so much so that it seemed she may burst into tears. Her dark, almond shaped eyes misted as she turned and retreated into a room Vlad recognized at once. A room in *his* castle.

His voice was a whisper. "Ioana is there now? In my Târgoviște castle?"

Mariela nodded. "She kept her promise to you. As I am sure you did to her, to the best of your ability."

"Forsaking all others," Vlad told his hands as they knotted together in his lap. "Until we can be married. Why is she here?"

Mariela shook her head. The golden coins on her *diklo* tinkled musically. "I cannot tell you such things, as I do not know. Perhaps, if God is willing, you will find out."

Vlad's heart thudded in his chest with a newfound fervor. Ioana, his Ioana, was there. As of yet unmarried, and there—in *his* castle!

"Now," Mariela said, "Ask the Lord, should He see fit, to show you troubles to come, so that you might recognize them."

Vlad looked from the old, toothless Gypsy back down into the crystal. "Troubles to come?"

Mariela nodded. "Perhaps it could be a prayer for wisdom, answered in advance."

Vlad did the sign of the cross. "*In Nomine Patris, et Filii, et Spiritus Sancti.*" He closed his eyes and Hail Mary after Hail Mary rolled off his tongue in Romanian. "*Bucură-te; Marie, cea plină de har, Domnul este cu tine, binecuvântată ești tu între femei, și binecuvântat este rodul trupului tău Isus. Sfântă Marie, Maica lui Dumnezeu, roagă-te pentru noi păcătoșii, acum și în ceasul morții noastre. Amin.*"

*Holy Mary, make me your vessel to protect your Son's teachings. Use these good Christian Wallachians to show me what it is that you would like me to see.*

*God, speak to me, your humble servant, and defender of your faith and your church on earth.*

When Vlad opened his eyes, Ioana had disappeared, and an image cleared in the crystal before him, like fog from the valleys in the early morning hours.

There he was, himself seated on his rightful throne of Wallachia, not much older than he was now. From the dark of the forest, two men in tall, white turbans emerged.

"Those are Turks." Vlad's voice was incredulous. "In my Wallachia!"

Together, still concealed by the tree line, they secreted weapons upon their persons as they drew nearer to the Târgoviște castle walls.

Vlad leaned forward intently.

When his castle doors were opened, the Turks were smiling, as were his Wallachian guards.

"They opened my castle's doors to Ottomans, and they did so under the guise of friendship." Vlad's eyes squinted. "Again, they lie."

"When have you known any Turk serving Murad to be truthful?" Mariela countered.

The image may have cleared from the crystal, but the ominous feeling that came with it still filled the small Gypsy camp. The message had been clear.

The Ottomans were coming for him.

## Capitol Treisprezece

Transylvanic Alps, Gypsy Camp
in the Year of our Lord, 1447

*Trust in the Lord with all your heart and do not lean on your own understanding.*

*~Proverbs 3:5*

Vlad knelt before the crucifix that marked the altar of the Transylvanic Gypsy camp and studied the distant horizon. The deep darkness that cloaked the land just before the sunrise blanketed the whole of Wallachia that he could see. Vlad, with the help of the Catholic Gypsies that claimed to be waiting for him in the mountains when he returned to Wallachia from his years of Ottoman bondage to Wallachia, had built the altar themselves while they waited on his arrival.

Mariela, the matriarch, had insisted the altar be constructed at the furthest east end of the camp, as it was the first place in camp to catch the rays of the rising morning sun, which made the entire altar even more spectacular.

They had constructed it from Catholic items spanning the world. Pieces of gems, rocks, and beads came from as far away as the Orient and England, while wood from olive trees and rose bushes came from the Holy Land itself.

The statue of Our Lady was Vlad's favorite part of the altar. Though beautiful as the Blessed Virgin always was, this particular statue depicted her as Our Lady of Sorrows. Jeweled swords, numbering seven in total, pierced the Mother of God's Sacred Heart as she sat in her red robe and blue mantle, her lovely face contorted in agony.

Vlad knelt before Jesus's mother and began to pray and meditate, just as he did every morning as the sun rose.

*First sorrow of the Blessed Mother. The prophecy of Simeon, where Simeon said he, already an old man, would not die until he saw the Lord's Christ.*

Vlad clasped his hands together atop the kneeler.

*As Simeon excitedly awaited Jesus, let me excitedly await the unfolding of Your Will for the reclamation of my throne.*

*Second sorrow of the Blessed Mother. The flight into Egypt.*

The smell of coffee boiling in the pot nearest the fire met his nose. Something about the scent of coffee was incredibly soothing.

*When Radu and I were traded to the Ottomans, did our mother, Vasilisa Maria, try to make flight into Ottoman territory to rescue us?*

*Third sorrow of Mary. The loss of Jesus and the finding of him in the Temple of Jerusalem.*

Vlad opened his eyes to check the sun. For a moment, when it peeked over the mountains, it caught the glass rosary beads and cast a heavenly glow over the east end of the camp.

*As Mary and Joseph sought twelve-year-old Jesus for three days before finding him back in Jerusalem, teaching the elders in the Temple, would Mother have rejoiced to find Radu and me? Chained in the dungeon? Father, unlike Saint Joseph, would not have accompanied his spouse, our mother, in her quest to find us. After all, it was Father who put us there.*

*Fourth sorrow of the Blessed Virgin. Mary's meeting Jesus on the Via Dolorosa.*

Sure enough, the sun caught the glass beads of the rosary and bathed Vlad in the heavenly blue, or *Marian blue*, as he had come to call it. *Would Mother's heart have commiserated with mine, when she found me locked in the dungeon? Would she have rescued me?*

*Fifth sorrow of Mary. The Crucifixion.*

Vlad glanced up at the centerpiece of the altar, the golden crucifix on which the silver body of Jesus Christ hung.

*Crucifixion. The most extended, painful, and perfected way to extract the most misery from a person before extracting their very life from their body. The Romans may have perfected crucifixion to a horrific art, but the Ottomans' brand of torture was certainly nothing to scoff at, either.*

*Sixth sorrow of the Blessed Mother. Jesus is taken down from the Cross.*

Vlad's mind drifted to the face of his mother. It was the last time he saw her, as he rode off with his father and Radu, bound for the Ottoman Empire on his father's death-dealing mission. She stood in her chamber's window in the soft early morning light. She was frowning, and it looked as though she had been crying. Still, Vlad had offered a wave to her, and she smiled and waved back.

*Would you have cried for me, Mother? If you are even still alive, are you crying over Radu?*

*Seventh sorrow of the Mother of God. The burial of Jesus by Joseph of Arimathea. Everything comes to an end. I cannot imagine burying Radu, how did the Blessed Mother feel as she buried her son? How would Mother feel burying Radu or me? Does she even know that her oldest son and husband are dead? Nobody mentioned her fate. . . is my mother dead, too?*

"I bring news," a breathless runner cried, successfully interrupting Vlad's morning meditations. "Life altering news, from the mouth of John Hunyadi himself."

Vlad stood and did the sign of the cross before turning from the altar. "Is that so? Pray tell, share your message with me."

The runner, a young Gypsy boy about Vlad's age, spoke quickly between whoops of breath. "Hungary and Transylvania have joined forces against Wallachia."

Vlad narrowed his eyes at the runner, who looked remarkably

similar to Mariela. A jumbled message of war, betrayal, Vladislav II, Hungary—Vlad.

Vlad listened silently then repeated the runner's message. "So, what you are telling me is that I shall not attack Vladislav as he sits on my rightful throne at Târgovişte—that the fight shall ultimately come to me? Am I hearing you correctly, Runner?"

He nodded, his hands on his knees as his breathing evened out. "My name is Lash, Your Grace. And yes, you heard me correctly. Vladislav, the pretender who sits on your rightful throne, has shown his horrific self and rallied his troops—those would be your troops—and turned them against John Hunyadi, King of Transylvania and Hungary."

"I see, Lash." Vlad crossed his arms and nodded thoughtfully. "Do we know why he chose to attack his ally?"

Lash lifted his head. He had three colored holes drilled into his front tooth, as did most of the Gypsies with whom he found himself. "Vladislav has no allies, Your Grace. Hungary is Wallachia's friend no more. Your uncle makes war with everyone. He said he will conquer the whole of Europe before he finds a worthy foe to stop him."

"I understand." Vlad rubbed his chin. "And how are our numbers? How many good Wallachian people stand behind our cause?"

Tamas appeared behind Lash. "We call ourselves Truth Seekers, Your Grace. And there are many. More every day. Many, many more not willing to live one more day under Vladislav's rule. Many more Wallachians who are willing to fight—and *die*—for you."

The image of Ioana in his castle window flashed into his mind. At once, he pushed it away. He could not think of her or her fate right now. Not while there were decisions to be made. Instead, he squatted and rubbed his hands together.

"Here is what we will do. We will sit. We will watch. Most importantly, we will wait."

Tamas pointed to a fiery sunrise beyond the altar. "Look there, Your Grace."

Vlad rose and studied the distant horizon. "That is no ordinary sunrise." He squinted then sniffed the air.

Tamas cleared his throat. "It appears as though the fight may come to us sooner than we expected."

"You are right." Vlad nodded. "That is a fire."

Lash stood, his hands on his hips. "That brings me to the remainder of the news, Your Grace."

Vlad turned to face him. "You mean there is more?"

Lash nodded. "Vladislav has gone on the attack. He is sacking and burning Saxon villages as he battles to take the whole of Transylvania."

"Just the Saxon villages?"

"Yes."

Vlad furrowed his brows. "Why?"

Lash shifted his weight. "Because it is the Saxons who resist him, Your Grace."

Vlad nodded. "I see. Does that conclude your news?"

Lash nodded but stopped. "Oh! I almost forgot." He reached into the inside of his vest and produced a folded piece of parchment. "He sent you a letter."

"Vladislav did?"

"No." Lash turned the letter over to reveal the Hungarian wax seal. "John Hunyadi did."

Curls of smoke reached over the treetops as Vlad accepted the letter. Hunyadi's wax seal ensured the letter was pure. He turned his back on his Gypsy counterparts and read it alone.

> *Vlad Drăculea, Rightful King of Wallachia,*
> *Rumors have reached Hungary that you have returned to Wallachia from the clutches of death to the south of our countries in order to claim your rightful throne. Both you and your brother, Radu, were thought to be dead, after your late father broke his alliance with the Ottomans. Now, it seems you are resurrected, much to the delight of not only*

*the Pope and the Holy Roman Empire, but to the whole of Christian Europe as well.*

*My spies tell me that you are camped in the woods, along with your ever-growing following of commoners, awaiting the perfect time to retake your God-given place as the rightful Voivode of Wallachia.*

*The common men of Wallachia, Transylvania, and Hungary want to see you on the throne, Vlad Drăculea. The question I have for you is this. Do you want the Hungarian military force to help you get there? Together, we can dispose of the pretender—and the ultimate failure as a person—your uncle, Vladislav II.*

*Please send word at your earliest convenience.*
*Your Natural Ally in Christ,*

*~John Hunyadi*

*P.S. During your absence, my illegitimate daughter, Ioana—I trust you remember her—was sent to your castle in order to serve as a Lady to your mother. Since things have taken an unexpected turn between our countries, no matter your decision on choosing to accept my help or not, I trust you will ensure her safety.*

Vlad folded the letter and stuck it into his inside breast pocket, over his thundering heart. "Mariela, please scribe for me."

The snaggle-toothed Gypsy stood before him, parchment and quill in hand. "I already know the words you will send to your natural ally, Your Grace."

Vlad's lips pulled up into a smile. "Is that so? Then what is it that you figure me to say?"

Mariela read from the paper she had already written.

*John Hunyadi, my natural ally in Christ,*
*Thank you for sending word. My advisors have informed*

me that I will sit on the Wallachian throne, much to the happiness of the whole of the Christian world, including the Holy Roman Empire, Transylvania, Hungary, and Wallachia. I humbly find your offer acceptable, to join forces against the pretender Vladislav II. Please send your emissaries so that we might plan a joint venture. Then, perhaps, we can speak of joining forces against the Sultan, as I have unfinished business south of the Danube.

Your ally in Christ,
~Vlad Drăculea III, Voivode of Wallachia

P.S. As soon as I find myself upon my throne and in a position to do so, I can assure you that your previous postscript request will be carried out, with eternal vows included, should it please you and the person of which we speak.

Mariela handed the letter to Vlad.

"When did you write this?"

She pretended to count on her fingers. "When you were caught escaping from Tokat Castle. By the little river, along the rocky outcropping."

Vlad pursed his lips. "And the camels?"

"They had not arrived yet. One had one hump, but the one you were strapped atop had two. But you know that story far better than I."

Vlad tried not to remember the hellish ride back to Tokat Castle following his thwarted escape. And the punishment that was exacted upon Andrei and Luca as a result of his capture.

"You truly are a gift from the Almighty, Mariela."

Vlad accepted the letter and signed it with her quill pen. "On several occasions, whilst I was in Ottoman captivity, I felt so incredibly alone. Especially once Radu submitted and accepted a place in court."

He looked into the twinkling eyes of the smiling Gypsy.

"Now I know that I was never alone. Thank you."

Mariela nodded as the smile faded suddenly from her wrinkled façade. "Remember, Voivode Vlad, not all Wallachians are true Christians. Some who should kiss your feet would do just that before stabbing you in the back at first chance."

Before Vlad could make sense of her puzzling words, the spry old Gypsy woman bowed and kissed his feet. When she rose, she held a dagger in her hand.

A resounding gasp from those who stood nearby was interrupted as a handful of confused Gypsy men drew their blades from their scabbards. Vlad's eyes widened as his trusted friend stood before him in the suddenly tense morning air, with a dagger pointed at his chest.

*She could kill me, should she try right now.* Vlad steeled his face, as he had when taking a beating from Ahmed. He folded the letter Mariela had penned, and handed it back to Lash, who ignored the goings on, accepted the letter, and disappeared into the surrounding forest. *But should she be successful, at least my blood would spill upon Wallachian soil.*

With so many pairs of poring eyes watching, waiting, and praying, to see what happened next, Mariela flipped the blade into the air and caught it expertly by the handle in her gnarled hand. She winked at Vlad. "Amen."

He accepted the dagger and ran his finger along the blade. Its cold steel was impossibly smooth and blemish free, until the end nearest the blade. Vlad ran his finger over the roughness before bringing it closer for a proper examination. "It has been engraved here."

"Is that so? What does it say?" Mariela's voice was much too innocent to be sincere regarding her ignorance of the dagger's engraving.

"It says—" Vlad's lips pulled back into a sincere grin. He chuckled. "For Vladislav."

The old Gypsy woman laughed alone until she was joined by a few more chuckles, then a few more, until the tension that had befallen the campsite was made a distant memory, the momentary distrust replaced at once by the warm friendliness as it had been before.

When the laughter died down, and everyone in the camp slowly returned to their own doings, Mariela erased the space between Vlad and herself. She dropped her voice so only he could hear. "Trust no one, Your Grace. Especially not now, since the fiery circle of fate and nobility has been awakened."

"Fiery, yes." Vlad sniffed the air again. "What do we know of the fires that are burning in the distance?"

Tamas, having overheard, chimed in. "Vladislav lights them, Your Grace. He burns Saxon villages to the ground and leaves them to smolder until they are reduced to ashes."

"Is there any danger of the fires spreading to the nearby forest?"

"Not at this time, Your Grace."

Vlad nodded. "I see. Once I am restored to the throne, I will see to it that the Saxons affected receive some restitution so that they may rebuild and move forward."

"We know you will, Your Grace." Tamas dropped his voice low. "We have some savings until then, Your Grace. Would you allow us to take some restitution to the villages in the meantime?"

Vlad's eyes widened at Tamas's generous offer.

"It is true," Mariela said, her eyes twinkling. "We have prepared for this for years."

"I humbly accept your generous offer." Vlad stretched his hand out to Tamas, who grabbed it in both of his. "I will return your money to you, once I am successfully restored."

"We know you will." Tamas shook his hand harder. "We know."

"Would you like to be the one to take the gifts to the villages, Tamas?"

The older man's dark eyes twinkled beneath his gray wool cap. "It would be my absolute honor to do so. When shall I leave?"

Vlad released his hand from their grasp. "At your pleasure and convenience is suitable to me."

Tamas wiped his hands on the front of his patchwork pants. "I would like to go as soon as possible then." He turned on his heel and dashed off to the direction of his *vardo*.

Mariela stood beside Vlad and nodded after her son. "God bless you, Prince Vlad Drăculea III, Voivode of Wallachia and Defender of the Faith. We have waited and prayed for your return."

Vlad looked sideways at the old woman, who may well have been an angel, and hefted the dagger. "Thank you for this gift." Vlad sank the deadly gift into his belt, alongside his dragon-crested blade. "When we leave for battle—" Vlad draped his arm around the shoulders of the grandmotherly old woman—"do say that you will come with me and stay at my side, as my most trusted advisor?"

"As you wish it, my lord." Mariela patted Vlad's arm with hearty thumps. "So will it be." Though her voice sounded reassuring, her face told a different story, a story Vlad could not entirely read.

# XIV

## Capitol Paisprezece

### Outside Târgovişte in the Year of our Lord, 1447

*Take pains with these things; be absorbed in them, so that your progress will be evident to all.*
*~1 Timothy 4:15*

*Vlad Drăculea, Rightful King of Wallachia,*
*How thrilled Hungary is to have her natural ally, Wallachia, back under Christian rule. She looks forward to assisting you however you might require, as you begin your ascent to your rightful throne. Your previous correspondence included no mention of your brother, Radu. Pray tell me, how is he?*
*Joining forces against another of our shared enemies will be a wonderful way to celebrate our victory against Vladislav II, as will the eternal vows of which you mentioned, and a permanent alliance of our two countries.*
*Two weeks from this day, we shall meet in the easternmost clearing near your current encampment, two hours before the dawn.*
*Please send word at your earliest convenience.*
*Your Natural Ally in Christ,*

*~John Hunyadi*

"Today is the day." Vlad spoke under his breath as he and his Wallachian rebel army, comprised of both common folk and ragtag Gypsies alike, crept out of the woods and into the clearing. He patted his pocket that held the most recent letter from John Hunyadi which stated the date, place, and time they were to meet and join the forces of Wallachia and Hungary.

Now, that time, place, and date had come.

A small prayer rolled off his lips. "God, remember us, your humble servants."

There, across the clearing, mostly shielded by the Wallachian understory, stood a larger military force than he was expecting. John Hunyadi stood out front, proudly sporting his Hungarian colors and his spiked golden crown. Vlad stepped out into the falling moonlight and waved.

Mariela's rickety voice was low, so only Vlad could hear. "Your following is coming together, Your Grace. But it has not finished growing yet."

John Hunyadi waved his arm high above his head, and his voice boomed across the clearing. "Welcome home, my friend!"

Vlad pulled his defenses back in and relaxed his face. He mirrored Hunyadi's wave. "Welcome to Wallachia!"

In tandem, the pair of rulers strode out toward the middle of the clearing. As they drew closer, Vlad stretched out his hand and caught Hunyadi's. At once, John pulled him into an embrace. A familial emotion washed over Vlad, something he had not felt in years. He embraced John back.

"Welcome back from the dead, Voivode," John said as he thumped Vlad's back in hearty pats. "Some people might think Vlad Drăculea III can rise from the dead at will," he joked. "Not only did your late father report your death to Wallachia, but the Ottomans did as well."

Vlad pulled back from their embrace. "Did they report Radu's as well?"

John shook his head. "There has been no word of Radu whatsoever.

Only that from your late father, who reported you both dead, having been, as he put it, *sacrificed for the good of Christendom*, I believe."

Vlad nodded. "It is refreshing to talk to a ruler who speaks the truth for a change."

"I am sure it is." John looped his arm over Vlad's shoulders. "Come. Let our armies intermingle. You and I have business to discuss."

"Business besides Vladislav?" Vlad waved to Mirela and Tamas, who yelled something in Romani to the misbegotten army. At once, the whole of the makeshift Wallachian army spilled into the clearing.

John also motioned to his side of the clearing. Hundreds, perhaps thousands, of Hungarian and Transylvanian soldiers marched into the clearing. Vlad looked—then looked again.

"They are all prepared to fight for your ascension to the throne, Vlad." John shifted his gaze from the unending sea of troops to a small tent set up on the barren field before them. "The other business would your mother—"

Vlad's breath hitched in his throat.

"And my daughter, Ioana."

†††

"This is it. This is where we will meet Vladislav's forces. He knows you are here, I fear, and he is backed by the boyars who killed your father and brother, as you may well know." John Hunyadi sounded wise in the pre-dawn chill.

"So I have heard," Vlad agreed.

The Hungarian king was taller than Vlad remembered him to be. He towered over most of his own men, which gave him even more of a commanding presence than he already possessed. Vlad wracked his brain for what few memories of Hunyadi he could muster, but his time in Ottoman hands squelched whatever memories they did not twist. What few he could summon to the forefront of his mind regarding Hunyadi were positive ones.

"My father and brother will be avenged, even though they dealt me into the hands of the devil without a second thought." Vlad's temper flared unexpectedly.

Hunyadi's hand came to rest on his shoulder. "It is good to have a true ally in Wallachia. You must know that your father not only double-crossed you, but he doubled-crossed me, too. Once we reinstate you to your throne," Hunyadi patted his shoulder before pulling his armor headpiece over his crown, "we will do as you requested in your letter and join forces against Mehmed II."

A younger, auburn-haired boy probably around Radu's age appeared at Hunyadi's side. "Voivode Vlad, meet Matthias, my son."

Vlad nodded.

"It is wonderful to have you on our side, Voivode Drăculea, and welcome home from the den of thieves." Mattias smiled. "If I may, what business in the Ottoman Empire will you and my father be going to settle, once you are back on your throne, of course?"

Vlad glanced at Hunyadi, who smiled. "My son, the future ruler. The best way to learn is by doing. So, Ally in Christ, if it proves not to be a bother to you, I should like Mattias to join us. As you and I both know, death comes for us all, and once it comes for me..."

"Father, you shall not speak of death. You know Mother asked you not to." Mattias leaned toward Vlad and lowered his voice. "She says it is bad luck to speak of such things and may even hasten them along."

"I see." Vlad shifted his weight. Should he have a son someday, he could see himself raising him on the field of battle, defending Christendom, much like Hunyadi and Mattias. "My business in Turkey is troubling. You see, I was left alone in the dungeons as a prisoner when my brother Radu abandoned the Faith, abandoned me, and abandoned the whole of Wallachia in favor of a room in the Turkish palace of Tokat Castle. So there he remains, by his own volition."

Mattias crossed himself. "The unforgivable sin."

Vlad nodded. "More importantly, two Wallachians boys, their

names are Luca and Andrei, were viciously blinded in my stead when I angered the Sultan."

"Those monsters!" Mattias's eyes were round as dinner plates. "And you wish to repatriate your countrymen?"

Vlad nodded again. "You are correct. Your father has taught you much about loyalty, I see."

Hunyadi displayed the the smile of a father, proud of his son.

*I wonder if I ever made my father proud in such a way as this?* Vlad shook off the unwelcome thought at once.

"Yes," John shook his head, "Mattias has learned well."

"Loyal friends and allies are the best kinds to have," Vlad added. "Rest assured, both of you, that you have an enduring friend in Wallachia as long as I am on the throne."

Hunyadi's brown eyes twinkled in the moonlight. "Then let us see to it that we get you there, Voivode Vlad."

Vlad glanced down to Mattias, then back to John. "I believe we had other matters to discuss as well, did we not?"

John jutted his strong chin in the affirmative and patted his son on the back. "Mattias, go see to it that the men are sufficiently watered. The riverbed was filled to the brink, so they should be. However, do run check."

"Certainly, Your Grace." Mattias turned and strode across the clearing in the early morning's light with the same brand of commanding steps as his father.

"He is certainly made from your image," Vlad said. "And you are raising him up fine."

John furrowed his brows. "Let us talk plainly. You wish to know news of your mother and of Ioana, do you not?"

"Straight down to business." Vlad tossed his black locks over his shoulder. "Yes, I do."

"Ioana, as you know, came to Wallachia as Lady in Waiting to your mother, Cneajna, as she was known to her friends. My daughter is there now, alone and unprotected, in the castle that the usurper calls his own."

Vlad stilled his movements so as to absorb every word Hunyadi had for him.

"Do you plan to marry her, as she planned to marry you before your rather sudden departure for the lands south of the Danube?"

Vlad lifted his chin. "If it be pleasing to Your Grace, and should Ioana consent to have me, then yes. I would stand proudly beside her as her bridegroom, before God and the good people of Wallachia, from now until eternity."

Vlad wanted so to tell John that it was thoughts of Ioana, tucked safely into the dark recesses of his mind, that helped him to endure the beatings. Endure the assaults. Endure the depraved years of a youth spent in vile captivity. However, for some reason, he held his tongue.

"Very well then. I shall work all the harder to help you to your throne." He nodded as though they had just reached a business agreement instead of a marriage contract. "Now onto the business of your mother."

Vlad tried not to look too eager, though his heart had ached for his precious mother, the former Princess of Moldavia, every moment of every day that he was away. He even had, on numerous occasions, found himself searching the faces of people coming and going from Tokat Castle, praying to find hers searching the faces of the people there, looking for his.

"She tried to come for you, Vlad. She tried to come for you and Radu." John's round eyes widened, and he leaned forward. "She sent envoys to follow you, as you left Wallachia in the company of Radu and your father. The envoys, all Moldavian by birth and more loyal to her than to the late Voivode, were assassinated at the border before they could cross." He paused and let this sink in for the new Wallachian leader. "She never stopped trying. She tried to come herself which caused such a scandal that your father sent her away."

"Sent her away?"

"Yes. To Transylvania, under lock and key, where she still remains to this day."

Vlad's shoulders hunched to his ears. "You are King of

Transylvania, why did you not do something?" His voice had grown louder, but he did not care.

John, unintimidated as a stone, lowered his voice further. "I did. I kept her safe from your father. He said if she threatened his peace with the Sultan, he would relieve her of her head himself." He leaned forward, effectively erasing any gap between them. "And he would have. I saved her life."

Vlad's fiery temper cooled as though he was a red-hot horseshoe that had just been thrust into the water barrel. He sucked in a deep breath and let it out slowly.

John continued. "Before I could free her, following your father's death, Vladislav turned on Hungary and Transylvania and attempted to make war. So I left her there, where she was safe. In exile more than as a prisoner."

Vlad opened his mouth to answer, or to apologize for his flash of temper, or to thank Hunyadi, but before he could, movement from across the eerily quiet field effectively silenced him.

Thoughts of his mother evaporated with the morning mist as, ever slow, Vlad drew his dragon-crested dagger from his belt. "Did your runner report the location of Vladislav's forces?"

Hunyadi nodded and drew his blade, as well. "Vladislav and his pack of raving boyars are still a hard day's ride away. They are coming, but not until tomorrow night at the earliest." Hunyadi paused. The wind in the trees seemed to whisper secrets to John that Vlad himself could not understand. "Whoever is out there now is not the enemy we await."

Radu's face burst into Vlad's mind without warning. The way his younger brother smiled smugly as sat with the Sultan, as a lover would sit, the day they were told of their father's assassination. *My last day under Ottoman rule.*

Radu may well have been Lucifer, prideful in the fact that he could never be cast from paradise. The blade trembled in Vlad's hand. *You are quick to forget, Radu, that even Lucifer was damned.*

"If it is not Vladislav..." The murderous red ring tinged the edges of Vlad's vision as he stared across the field, black hatred in his eyes. "Then it must be Turks."

Hunyadi nodded and pointed his sword toward the noise. "On three, we charge."

"Show no mercy," Vlad seethed. "We fight to win. And if we die, we die with honor. On Wallachian soil."

"One..."

Vlad motioned to his faithful followers. The sharp sound of steel being drawn from out of a forestful of sheaths sang out like a murderous falcon, hungry for blood.

Hunyadi sucked in a breath. "Two..."

Vlad's muscles twitched as every miserable night he spent in Turkish custody rolled through his mind like slow torture. Muscles that endured so many beatings, so much agony, so many unthinkable acts. Now, those same muscles burned for revenge.

"Three!"

Before the battle cry could erupt from their throats, a roughshod man brandishing a pitchfork stepped out of the tree line. "Hallo there! We be friend, not foe!

Vlad, Hunyadi, and the forces that pledged to fight with them charged a few feet, then stopped as more and more pitchfork-wielding villagers—a conglomerate of men, women, and children—joined the first man.

Vlad's jaw went slack as he tried to make sense of what he was seeing.

"We are the Saxons," the man flailed his pitchfork as he continued, "left homeless by Vladislav. It was the smoke of our burning homes you smelt, and the flames of our burning homes you saw with your own eyes." Still, he waved his pitchfork wildly.

"Ah yes," Vlad said, hoping he sounded as though he was in complete control of the situation. Which he was not.

"We received your gifts of restitution. Now, each of us have come to fight, and to die, for the rightful heir to the throne, Vlad Drăculea III!"

Vlad and Hunyadi strode across the battlefield, stepping in tandem, until they effectively closed the space in the clearing between them and the Saxons with careful, regal steps. When they reached the horde of yellow-haired people, Vlad saw that the man with the pitchfork was smiling.

"They call me Aldwyn. It means *old friend*, and you will find it to be true." The large man with dirty blond hair streaked with gray was dressed in tattered clothes. He greeted Vlad with a hearty clap on the back. "All of us here be homeless and destitute because of Vladislav."

A throng of fair-complected people surrounded Aldwyn, Vlad, and Hunyadi, who was smiling. Downtrodden women with dirt-streaked faces brandished pitchforks, while sour-faced children stared on from behind tree trunks and shrubs, makeshift clubs and stabbing implements clasped in their little hands.

"Every last one of you?" Vlad studied his displaced subjects. "Victims of Vladislav?"

Aldwyn stuck his pitchfork into the ground and accepted a mug of ale from an angry-looking woman with knotted hair. "Our villages were routed and burned. There was rape. There was torture. But most of all, wherever Vladislav went, bloody murder trailed him. Like a vulture."

A low grumble rumbled through the understory as others began to recount amongst themselves the atrocities which Vladislav had committed against them, their families, and their homes. Aldwyn stared at Vlad and continued. "He took more than our lives, you see. He tried to take our very will to live."

Those Saxons who found themselves nearby stopped talking amongst themselves quietly and listened to Aldwyn. They murmured in agreement as he spoke.

"Our will to live, and to fight, returned when we heard about your means to battle him with the help of John Hunyadi and retake your throne. Though it was Hunyadi himself who put Vladislav on the throne to begin with."

John held up his hands in mock defeat. "And rest assured, good Wallachian people, that is something that would have never happened, had I known that the true heir. . ." He put his hand over Vlad's head and raised his voice, "had I known that the information spread by both the Wallachians and the Ottomans was false, and the true heir to the Wallachian throne still lived!"

Aldwyn gave John a sideways look before continuing. "You will find us to be but a poor and homeless lot, but rich we are in loyalty, courage, and cunning ability. We would rather die under your command, Vlad, than live under another day under Vladislav's."

A raucous roar went up from the unkempt lot as a gloomy woman, with white scars showing through the cakes of dirt on her face, pressed a mug into Vlad's hand. Her blonde hair stood out from her head in haggard mats like rays from the midday sun.

"And you, Madame? Why are you here?"

Aldwyn dropped his voice low. "She has more cause than most to join the fight against Vladislav."

Vlad drew a long drink of hot ale from the steaming mug. He raised his eyebrows at the woman. "Is that so?"

"Aye. Aye, it is." Her voice was scratchy, as though she had a cold. A skinny boy, missing both of his front teeth, peeked out from behind her threadbare skirts. "When Vladislav marched through our village, my family hid in the barn. We knew what would happen if we were discovered. They used hounds, hounds to sniff us out. They found me first."

Vlad looked around at the faces of the women who had gathered around them. They nodded along as the woman spoke.

"I was raped in front of my husband and in front of my son. I was also pregnant." She waited to continue until Vlad stopped gazing about and looked her dead in the eye, instead. She never turned her deadpan stare from his as she told her story in a monotonous voice. "They took turns having a go at me, they did, and each one of those murderous devils were rougher than the one before. So rough."

Moisture pooled in her clear, blue eyes, but did not fall. "They killed my unborn child, another boy. He was born dead between Vladislav's soldiers as they did their devilish deeds with my body. They left me for dead—probably figured I was—then Vladislav himself came forward. He took out his sword and murdered my husband." She reached back and absently stroked her son's head. "My son would have been killed, had he not hidden in the potato sacks filled with rotten peelings in the deepest part of the barn."

Vlad's heart went out to her. He, better than anyone, understood what she had endured. "My dear lady—" he began, but she cut him off and continued.

"They set my home ablaze. Barn too. We got out and hid with the hogs." She swiped her nose with the back of her hand. Her stare, though watery, was hard as stone and hot with hate. "Tried to get my husband's body out. Baby too." She shook her head. "We could not. They burned with the barn."

Silence covered the lot of them like a funeral shroud.

She sniffled back any emotion that threatened to overflow and continued. "Vladislav took everything from me. Now I want to take everything from him. Or die trying."

Vlad drained the contents of his mug and returned it to the scar-faced lady. "Revenge is a powerful motivator, and you have lost much. In time, perhaps we can both come to see that forgiveness will be more powerful."

*Forgive us our trespasses as we forgive those who trespass against us.*

Her eyes were flinty. "Then I shall forgive his damned soul after we kill Vladislav and the rightful voivode is returned to his throne." She cupped her hands around her mouth and let out a yell. "All hail the Voivode! All hail Vlad Drăculea, Voivode of Wallachia!"

A ring of Saxons began to chant, their pitchforks raised high. "All hail Vlad! All hail Vlad Drăculea!"

Vlad raised his hand. At once, the masses quieted. He looked into the Saxon woman's flinty eyes. "You have as much courage as any man I have ever met. Come. Fight with us against Vladislav and the traitorous boyars that murdered your former Voivode and prince."

Finally, the woman's dirty face cracked into a bent smile. She nodded. The wild cheering that echoed through the Wallachian forest from the cheering Saxons made it sound as though their following had more than doubled in but a moments time.

# Capitol Cincisprezece

### Wallachia
### in the Year of our Lord, 1448

*When I was a child, I used to speak like a child, think like a child, reason like a child; when I became a man, I did away with childish things.*

*~1 Corinthians 13:11*

Mariela's face was grim when she met Vlad at his tent the next morning. "This morning, you will see much death, Voivode Vlad."

He pulled on his shirt and glanced at the sun as it peeked over the horizon. "With Vladislav? We are not due to meet his forces until tonight. Are we not?"

Mariela, normally smiling, refused to lift her lips from their downcast position. "News of your return has spread quickly. Vladislav is coming here with murder in his eye. Now. And he has sworn that he will take your head off himself and place it on a stake outside of *your* castle."

"He shall not succeed." Vlad rubbed his chin. "Mariela, when are these troops set to arrive?"

"Late morning. Possibly mid-day."

Vlad nodded. "Have we informed Hunyadi of the change?"

The nearby stream babbled to the tune of early morning birdsong. "No, Your Grace. I came to you first."

Vlad began to button his shirt. "Pray, do tell my natural ally of the change in our circumstance." He paused. "Would you do something else for me, as well?"

"Of course."

Vlad gazed into the distance. "We have no priest in camp. I have not taken Holy Communion in years, as we were not afforded the luxury of the Sacraments as non-believers in Turkey." He turned to face Mariela. "Before we do battle today, would you help me to renew my baptismal promises with Wallachian water?"

The old woman's forlorn face cracked into a broad smile.

"I was christened as a child," Vlad explained, "but to renew my baptismal promises, on Wallachian soil, with Wallachian water, after my Turkish ordeal ..."

Mariela raised her hand to stop his needless explanations and reasonings. "It would be my honor, Your Grace."

"Well done, then. Do go speak with Hunyadi, and then I will meet you at the river's edge."

With a nod, Mariela disappeared from the mouth of the tent. Vlad finished his buttoning and stepped outside in her wake. Nearby, the clan of Saxons tended the camp's fires. Meat, with aromatic fat dripping into the flames, sizzled. He licked his lips. Some of the Saxon women had already began serving mugs of ale to anybody who passed by, be that person Hungarian, Transylvanian, Gypsy, or Wallachian.

A few women stooped over the fires and removed the sizzling meat. He watched as they served all who were hungry, sometimes to the tune of laughter. Many smiles were in camp, and that did Vlad's heart good.

*Thank you, Father. Not only have I been freed from Ottoman bonds, but you led me to freedom when I felt certain I would never be free again. Each day to live free and Christian ... it is worth fighting to preserve, Father. Thank you for my warrior's heart and for blessing me with being able to fight for Christendom.*

Vlad prayed as he meandered through camp on his way to the river, an otherworldly peace filling in his heart.

*Father, please keep Your hand over Luca and Andrei and the rest of the Wallachian boys in Ottoman captivity. Please help them hold on and do not let them lose faith. Please, if it be Your Will, assure them that they are not forgotten. Assure them, Father, that I am coming for them. Amin.*

As the prayer ended, Vlad found himself at the river's edge. Slowly, he slipped off his shirt and hung it on a nearby branch. "Mariela should be here any moment now."

He squatted down and sunk his hands into the icy water. Forming his fingers into a bowl, he lifted it to his lips and drank in long swills from the crisp river. Birds sang their morning songs high in the treetops.

For the first time in years, Vlad's heart was light.

*Today, I reclaim my throne.*

Suddenly, as if on an unheard cue, the birds squelched their songs. From somewhere nearby, a twig snapped. "I thought I had finished the Drăculești line when I poisoned your father and tortured your brother to death."

Vlad froze, his fingers still cupped around his mouth. He did not recognize the voice that seethed like venom through the faceless lips, still concealed by the trees.

"I heard the rumor that you still lived. I heard that you somehow had the audacity to build an army and try to battle Vladislav II for the throne of Wallachia."

Slowly, Vlad dropped his cupped hands from his lips until one fell upon his dagger. The words engrained there burst to the forefront of his mind.

*For Vladislav.*

"No, there is no need for that." A tall man with dark hair and a voice like velvet, stepped out of the tree line opposite where Vlad squatted. "You see, there is no use in fighting. Because, as you and I both know, I will emerge the victor."

The man turned slightly, revealing a long, curved cutlass in his hand. "I will kill you, Vlad Drăculea III. I will kill you like I killed your father and like I killed your brother before you." He snickered. "However, it seems I will not be afforded the time to enjoy it, as I enjoyed killing them."

Vlad kept one hand on his dagger and slowly rose to his feet. "Who are you?"

"Since I aim to kill you, you should know the name of the man who does so." He held the cutlass out before him. "Be it known here and now that Roman Snagov of Wallachia helped relieve—"

*Snagov?* Vlad tightened his fingers around his dagger's handle. "What I have I done to incur your hatred?"

"You are a Drăculeşti. I will erase your line from this earth." With a roar, he splashed through the river, his arm outstretched and with rage boiling behind his eyes. "And save a thousand Wallachian boys in doing so."

Vlad unsheathed his dagger as someone behind them gasped. He tilted his head infinitesimally toward the sound, a novice error that provided just the opening that Roman needed. Before he could see who was behind him, the murderous boyar's blade was pressed to his throat.

"Do not do it, Roman." Mariela's voice was steady. Twigs snapped as she crept up to where the duo stood. "Vlad Drăculeşti has the answers you seek. The answers you would—and have—killed for."

Roman's trembling hand stilled. "What do you know about anything, old woman?" The sharp end of the blade cut into Vlad, and a drop of blood trickled down his neck. "And what do you know about what answers I seek?"

Her voice remained steady. "I know you would kill to have your son, Luca Snagov, returned to you from Ottoman hands."

"Luca!" Vlad could not keep the surprise from his voice. "That is where I recognized your name. Luca Snagov!"

The blade relaxed against Vlad's neck. "What did you say?"

"Luca." Vlad sheathed his dagger. "Your son is a true son of

Wallachia." Reaching up to the deadly cutlass blade, he shoved it away with both hands. Instead of battling Roman, Vlad turned and faced his tormentor. "Despite all that Luca and I endured together in the dungeon of Tokat Castle, torture and worse at the hands of the Ottomans, he never submitted to the Turks, never even thought about it. Even though life would be easier for him, and for me, had we just bent to their ill will. As my brother Radu did."

Roman, blade still clutched in his hand, stumbled backward. Tears pooled in his eyes and extinguished the fiery hate that had moments before burned there. His mouth moved but made no sound.

"Is that why you agreed to take part in a coup that not only overthrew, but killed my father and brother, Roman? Because they traded Wallachian boys to the Turks?" Vlad stepped toward him, and Roman did not move.

Vlad continued. "Luca not only remained loyal to God, Roman, but he remained loyal to Wallachia. Because the Ottoman Empire is a place where loyalty is rewarded with punishment, Luca was kept in the dungeon with me as a result. Because like your brave son, I also refused to submit to the Turkish ways."

"Tell me," Roman managed. Pain strained his voice and tears dripped heavily down his cheeks. "How is my son?"

"Sultan Mehmed II blinded Luca and another true Wallachian named Andrei to punish me, because they remained loyal to me. Not to them." Vlad held both of his hands out before him, welcoming, as a father would to his heartbroken child. "I promised Luca I would free him from those Ottoman devils. And that is my first goal, once I regain my rightful throne from my uncle Vladislav."

"Blinded?" Roman dropped his forgotten cutlass into the river and dug his fingers into his dark curls. If pain had a face, Vlad knew he looked upon it now. Roman crumpled, as though the ability to hold himself upright had been sapped from his body. "They blinded my son?"

Mariela patted Vlad on the arm with her gnarled hand. With a knowing look, she gestured toward the water. Vlad glanced at

Roman, who appeared to have completely forgotten he was there, and followed the old Gypsy woman into the deepest part of the river. "*In nomine Patris, et Filii, et Spiritus Sancti.* Do you, Vlad Drăculea, as a son of Wallachia and Defender of the Faith, renew your baptismal promise to spend your life rejecting the devil and all of his false promises, and do you do so in the name of the Father, and of the Son, and of the Holy Spirit?"

"I do." Vlad allowed her to guide him under the water and back up again. When he rose, a tear-stained Roman stood over him. Something glowed in his face that Vlad could not quite place.

*Roman, decide now. Are you friend or are you foe?*

After what seemed an eternity, Roman spoke, but did not move from his hovering stance. "If I should help you in your cause to regain the throne of Wallachia from Vladislav II, will you in turn permit me to lead the charge to liberate my son from the Ottoman Empire?"

Vlad rubbed the water from his eyes. "Your son has the heart of a warrior and the loyalty of which I have never seen. Did he inherit those traits from you, Roman?"

"Yes." Roman dipped to one knee and bowed his head before Vlad. River water parted and curled around him, but Roman paid it no mind. "I pray that you give me what your father refused me—nothing more than the chance to rescue my child."

Vlad bent down and plucked Roman's cutlass from the water. Slowly, he lowered it onto each of Roman's shoulders. Still, the older man's head remained bowed.

Vlad's voice escaped his lips in a hiss. "I could strike off your head now, in retaliation for you murdering my father and my brother."

"I pray you do, if you should not see fit to grant my request." Roman did not lift his head. "Do not force me to remain helpless in a world where I cannot even give my life to save my son's."

"Roman Snagov, fight with me for Christendom against Vladislav II. Then together, we shall liberate Luca and *all* of Wallachia's sons from Ottoman hands, so never will a Wallachian suffer their wrath again."

Tamas burst from the understory, breathless, as Roman rose from water. He stood, unashamed, and wiped tears that refused to be staunched from his eyes.

Tamas ignored Roman and looked at Vlad through wide eyes. "Vladislav has arrived. It is time."

Vlad, still standing in the water, offered Roman his cutlass. "Vladislav is here," he declared. "It is time to take back Wallachia." His hand fell to the dagger that hung on his own hip. The engraved dagger, the one meant for Vladislav. The time had finally arrived to use it.

Roman accepted his cutlass and raised his blade high. "For Vlad Drăculea, Voivode of Wallachia!"

## Capitol Saisprezece

### Wallachia
### in the Year of our Lord, 1448

*They will stumble repeatedly; they will fall over each other. They will say, 'Get up, let us go back to our own people and our native lands, away from the sword of the oppressor.'*
*~Jeremiah 46:16*

The smell of fire met Vlad's nose even before he saw Vladislav's army.

*Tactics, tactics, tactics. Setting fires so you come blazing into battle.* Vlad slipped his shirt back on and strode easily back to the clearing with Mariela, Tamas, and Roman following close behind.

*Well done, Uncle. But you will need more than flames to beat me today.*

The cacophony of horse's hooves rumbled in the Wallachian brush like biblical thunder. Vlad was immediately put in a mind of the Battle of Jericho, when sound alone brought down the fortress walls. *All they needed was to keep the faith.*

Hunyadi stepped to Vlad's side. "They are on horseback. If they have lances..."

Vlad glanced around. *This is my country.*

He thought quickly. "Instruct your men to climb the trees." Vlad spun on his heel and spoke to Mariela and Tamas. "Pray tell everyone you can find to climb the trees and to make haste in doing so. When Vladislav arrives, we will not be here. At least, we will not be seen."

Mariela did the sign of the cross in Vlad's direction. "God be with you, True Voivode of Wallachia."

"If God is with us, who could be against us?" He smiled. "Do hide yourself away from the battlefield, unless you feel you can climb a tree, too."

The old Gypsy smiled as the din grew louder and louder still. "I may surprise you. Now go, worry not about me, and win back your throne."

Vlad glanced around the clearing as all of his soldiers, those of Hunyadi, and those of the Saxons each shimmied up the branches and into the treetops. The din grew louder and louder until finally, Vladislav and his pack of raving boyars topped the distant hill. Vladislav was in the lead.

Vlad peered from between the branches and leaves. There were no more birdsongs, no more laughter. There was no sound aside from the galloping of horses and the crackling of none-too-distant fire.

*Vladislav, you think you are coming for me. But I have been waiting for this moment for many, many years.* Vlad gritted his teeth and drew his engraved dagger from its sheath. *Prepare to meet God and answer for your all of betrayals and for your transgressions against your blood.*

Vladislav did not slow his horse, nor did any of his boyars, as they road with a roar into the clearing.

Surprisingly, Vladislav's following was not nearly as large as he expected it to be. Vlad narrowed his eyes and watched as Vladislav, confused, slowed his horse when he realized there was no enemy to meet and defeat.

The pretender circled his horse through the clearing.

*You fool. You prideful fool. You just rode beneath the whole of the Hungarian army!*

Vladislav spoke to the boyars, and each in turn shrugged their shoulders and commenced to looking around, pointed to the still smoldering campfires that the Saxon women had tended and shook their heads.

"It is as though they simply vanished," Vladislav said.

*His voice sounds different than I remember.*

Vladislav motioned to the boyars. Each of them dismounted their horses. Their soldiers to follow suit. "Tie your horses in the tree line," Vladislav called. "Then take whatever you can. Cowards that they are, they must have turned tail and run."

His uncle handed his horse's reins to the first boyar to whom he spoke and motioned to the vicinity of Vlad's tree. The boyar was a man that Vlad recognized, but he could not call to mind his name.

He stopped right beneath him.

*This is it.*

"Now!" Vlad roared as he leaped from the tree, the dagger outstretched. Many of the boyars had started to lash their horses to occupied trees as well. Once Vlad gave the signal, soldiers of every Christian country that had come together to stand in defiance of tyranny began to rain down out of the trees upon the traitors, like hell's fire.

Vlad grasped the boyar's head and easily slit his throat with the dagger and let his body fall to the ground. *For Mircea*, he thought. *You, traitorous boyar, deserved much, much worse than the quick death I gave you.*

On the ever-widening battlefield, which was becoming smokier by the moment, the Wallachian rebels did the same. Catching boyars, slitting their throats.

Vlad studied the clearing. *Come on Vladislav, where are you. Show yourself.* He side-stepped the bodies as they fell, compliments of his army, as he searched for his missing uncle. *This battle is not over until I kill you.*

Hazy smoke settled thick over the battlefield as he crept through the trees that ringed the clearing. All of the sudden, Hunyadi's voice rang out above the moans and the groans, and the clashes and the clangs. "Behind you!"

Vlad did an about face but saw nothing.

"See him? Kill him!"

He squinted, but the gray veil of smoke proved too thick. He may as well have been blind. Vladislav burst forth through the smoky haze with a roar, as easily as he would dash through a silken curtain.

Vladislav looped his arm around Vlad's neck and yanked hard. Vlad fumbled his dagger and lost his grip. Thankfully, he did not drop it.

"You little whelp," Vladislav growled. "You have not a clue how many nights I stood over you and your brat brothers, thinking how easy it would be to secure my place on the throne of Wallachia if only you were dead." He squeezed hard and Vlad gasped for air. "Now that I have your fool father out of the way, and Mircea, the throne is mine."

Vlad tried to pretend he was holding his breath for fun, as he and Radu used to do, but the world went hazy, and it had nothing to do with the smoke. His mind drifted, as Vladislav seethed venomous words into his ear, back to a time when he thought his uncle Vladislav was his best friend. He loved to tag along with him when he worked with his horses in the stables. Sometimes, he would even lift Vlad and let him sit atop his fine steeds. Other times, when he came back from a ride, he would pass the brush to Vlad as though he was passing a bottle of drink to a man. *It is important to always brush out your horses. They rely on you*, Vladislav had wisely imparted as, together, they brushed out a lathered Arabian stallion.

*All that time, he was looking to kill me and wishing me dead, as I trailed him like a love-struck yearling. It is too bad that the horse that kicked his knee did not kick him in his head, then I would not find myself in this predicament now.*

Vlad's mind hung on that rogue, stable-bound memory.

Vladislav had been out riding during a visit to Targoviste. Vlad's father had made Vladislav a gift of that very spirited Arabian stallion. If you walked too close behind him, as Vladislav learned, the stallion was apt to strike out with a well-placed hind hoof.

*Which is why Vladislav walks with a slight limp to the left. His right knee...*

Vladislav's voice sounded far away. "As much as I wanted to kill you, it was not near as much as I wanted to bed your mother. She turned me down, you know, in favor of your fat father. As soon as I kill you, I am riding straight to Transylvania to do just that."

Lungs burning and with darkness closing in, Vlad lifted his right leg and kicked back as hard as he could. He landed his kick squarely to Vladislav's knee, which answered his kick with a *pop*.

The grip on his neck loosened as Vladislav fell to the ground with an agonized groan. Vlad adjusted the grip on his dagger but did not say a word. There was nothing to say anyway, as his uncle was no longer his family. He was a deadly stranger who threatened his life and his country and must be destroyed.

When Vladislav fell, the soupy smoke concealed him at once.

Vlad stabbed wildly into the smoke.

Nothing.

He stabbed again.

Still nothing.

Heart pounding, he kicked out wildly, searching for his foe.

*I cannot fail now!*

The toe of his boot met a body and elicited a groan from the fallen man.

*Aha! I got you now!*

Without a second thought about the man he once loved and idolized, the man he called uncle, the man he trusted, Vlad hefted his dagger above his head. Like a flash of lightning, he brought the dagger down hard. It sunk deep into the man's body and jammed into a bone. Vlad kept one hand on the dagger and waved the smoke from around the man with the other.

*Have to make sure you are dead...*

As the smoke curled away, Vlad's face contorted from relief into horror. The man he impaled with his dagger wore a flowing white robe and a tall turban.

*Ottomans!*

Vlad glanced up, suddenly filled with dread. *Why are the Ottomans here? And where is Vladislav?* Just as his eyes began to adjust to the low light offered by the haze, another Turk appeared through the smoky shroud.

His eyes locked on Vlad's, and he raised a curved cutlass with an ornately jeweled handle.

Vlad tugged on his dagger, which was firmly embedded in the dead man's breastbone. Nothing. He tugged harder.

Still nothing.

Forgetting the dagger, his hand went to his dragon crested sword. But it was too late. The Ottoman that stood before him brought his cutlass crashing down. Vlad closed his eyes and waited for death. Beside him, one of Vladislav's boyars crumpled to the ground, with an Ottoman cutlass fixed firmly in his skull.

Vlad's eyes widened as the Turkish soldier placed his foot on the boyar's head and yanked back hard. He then offered a nod to Vlad before disappearing back into the smoke.

*He just saved my life?!*

Before he could ponder on it further, Roman's voice rang out. "Here, I have him! I have Vladislav!"

Vlad reached down and, placing his foot against the dead Turk's chest and yanked his engraved dagger free before rushing off toward the sound of Roman's voice. He found him rolling on the ground, embroiled in a knife fight with a man sporting long, curly black hair.

*Uncle Vladislav.*

Roman's arms shook as he held Vladislav's blade-wielding hand, the dagger only inches from Roman's face.

"Kill him!" Roman cried.

Vlad hefted his dagger for the second time and brought it down, hard, right in the middle of Vladislav's back. Blood sprayed across Vlad's face, hot and wet. He swiped it as Hunyadi jogged up to him. "It is over. The boyars that are left are fleeing." He looked down at the body before them. "And it appears you took out Vladislav. Well, you and Roman."

John grabbed Vlad's hand and clasped them together. Quickly, he raised them, in a show of unity between their two countries, and loosed a victory cry. Vlad joined in, long and loud. Soldiers in their army answered with a triumphant howl until the understory, moments before filled with clanging steel and death moans, was alive with the sound of success.

The Saxon woman with the scarred face jogged over, her son only a step or so behind her. Like Vlad, her face was dotted with scarlet, and she held a bloodied blade in her hand. "Did you kill the pretender?"

Vlad motioned down at the body, which still lied before them, face down.

"I want to spit in his face," the woman said. She turned him over with her foot and leaned down, making a hacking sound in the back of her throat. As she arched her neck, she suddenly stopped. She swallowed hard and gave the body a hard kick. "It is not him. Not the pretender."

Vlad's face fell and something icy gripped his backbone. "Split up!" he cried. "Search the bodies. Vladislav has to be here. Somewhere."

†††

Hunyadi and Vlad met in the middle of the clearing. "Any sign of him?"

Vlad shook his head. "No. You?"

Hunyadi pursed his lips. "He does not seem to be here among the dead."

Vlad shrugged. "At least not now. But he will be."

"That he will." The Hungarian king motioned toward the castle, looming in the distance. "However as you said, he is not here now. And I do believe we have promises to keep, Voivode of Wallachia."

Vlad sucked in a breath through his nose and smiled. "That has quite the ring to it."

Hunyadi put his arm over Vlad's shoulder. "Speaking of rings, I believe we have a wedding to plan. In addition to becoming the Voivode of Wallachia, tonight you also become my son-in-law."

Heat crept into Vlad's neck and burned there. "If she will have me."

"Shall we go find out?"

Vlad nodded, and they started off toward the castle at a lope.

†††

Vlad and John stood on the other side of the moat from Targoviste Castle in silence and waited for the drawbridge to come down. As it did, she came into view. Vlad's breath caught in his throat. He coughed.

"She has gotten even more beautiful since the last time I saw her."

John stood with his hands behind his back. "The last time you saw her, you were children. Now you are a man—and she is a woman, fully ripe."

"She waited for me? She truly did?" Vlad took in the sight of her. Her onyx hair, much longer now, trailed down her back in loose curls, and her eyes, almond-shaped and seafoam green, burned with an intensity that he could almost feel, even from across the moat. Her lips, salmon pink against her olive skin, turned up into a teasing smile at the corners. "I cannot tell you how her memory, or thoughts of her memory, kept me going during my—"

Vlad bit off his words. *No. Not today.* Not today would he allow the thoughts of Tokat Castle and all of the goings on that happened there enter his mind. He glanced at John, who nodded.

"Of course she waited for you. She loves you. Anyway, she was the only person I could truly count on to keep a promise once it was made."

He stared at Vlad until the younger man met his gaze. "Until now."

The drawbridge creaked and fell the last couple of inches. Vlad let his gaze travel from Ioana to the castle's façade. The last time he had seen it, he was leaving his beloved castle, bound for Turkey. Up there was his old nursery window. The same one he had looked down from to see Mircea waving back at him. He glanced over his shoulder. The hanging tree, though partially obscured by a freshly constructed stone wall, still stood. A silent reminder of a life that had been, but was no more.

John coughed, bringing Vlad out of his unexpected daydream. "Shall we?"

The young voivode's heart thundered in his chest, and his palms went clammy as his stare fell immediately back to Ioana.

John Hunyadi gave a little bow. "After you, m'lord. This is your castle; you have earned this walk."

"You are right." Vlad puffed his chest and strutted across the drawbridge, straight towards Ioana. Straight towards his castle. Straight towards his reign as voivode. Straight towards everything he had dreamed about for the last five years, everything he knew he would never see again.

*By the Grace of God, I made it.*

# Capitol Saptesprezece

### Targoviste Castle, Wallachia in the Year of our Lord, 1448

*Love is patient, love is kind. It does not envy, it does not boast, it is no proud. It does not dishonor others, it is not self-seeking, it is not easily angered, it keeps no records of wrongs. It does not rejoice over wrongdoing but rejoices with the truth. It bears all things, believes all things, hopes all things, endures all things.*

*~Corinthians 13:4-7*

Ioana sunk into a deep curtsy as Vlad approached her. "Welcome home to what is already yours, Your Grace."

Her voice had grown sweeter over the years, like wine, aging to perfection in a barrel. It was so sweet that it left Vlad intoxicated, so much so that he was unable to respond.

Hunyadi stepped up beside him, thankfully, as she rose from her curtsy. "Hello, Daughter." He opened his arms wide. Ioana dashed into them at once. "I trust my son and your brother, Mattias, made it back here unscathed?"

Ioana nodded. "He did. He is asleep in my room."

"Was he worried?"

She shook her head. "Not at all. He said between you and Vlad

Drăculea III, the rightful heir to the Wallachian throne, no harm would dare to seek out either of you." She ventured a peek at Vlad before turning her attention fully back to her father. "And my prayers are answered because of it," she added quietly.

Finally, Vlad found his voice. "Shall we inside?" He mentally admonished himself for his lack of control of his own language. How grateful he was when neither John nor Ioana laughed as he led them inside, to the castle grounds that he could not wait to revisit.

"So where would you like to go first?" John asked as he strode along with Vlad and Ioana.

Before Vlad could speak, she cleared her throat. "I wager a guess that I know." She glanced up at the sun as it crept across the sky and toward the horizon and pointed. "Since it is not prime hunting time, my wager is that you wish to visit your chapel."

Vlad stopped walking so abruptly that John stumbled to keep from running into him. Ioana, however, did not. She stopped with him in tandem, as though they shared one mind. "Just as when we were children," Vlad marveled. "You seem to know my mind as if it is your own."

His eyes softened as he looked at her—he could feel it, and a genuine smile haunted his lips. He reached for her hand. "Would you accompany me to the chapel? There is much to be grateful for."

She allowed him to take her hand. "No."

Vlad stopped smiling. "No?"

Ioana shook her head. "I cannot go to the chapel with you now."

Behind them, John said nothing. But there, beneath the stone archways of the castle he so dearly loved and missed, Vlad's heart threatened to break within his very chest.

He cleared his throat but did not take back his hand. He could not, even if he had wanted to. Five years of waiting came down to this moment here. No matter if she did not love him anymore, he would have to face that truth later. Not today. And not now. For now, he simply could not let her go. Not yet.

Vlad cleared his throat again, but the sudden knot that had risen there threatened to strangle him. "May I ask why not?"

Ioana's eyes sparkled. "It seems someone has prepared the chapel for a wedding."

Vlad's eyebrows knitted above his eyes.

"Who ordered such a thing?"

"I did." Ioana tightened her fingers around his. "You promised that, when you returned home, you would never leave me again. I figured if we were married . . ."

Vlad did not realize his palms had dried until they began to sweat once again. He resisted the urge to yank his hand from hers and wipe them feverishly on his pants.

"I figured if we were married," she repeated, "you could never get away again. If you will have me, that is."

Vlad was at a loss for words.

Ioana, dressed in a flowing white dress with white lace *mantilla* around her neck beneath her hair, released Vlad's hand, ever gentle. "Oh Vlad. I am so sorry. I, I—"

She stammered over her words and began to back up across the cobblestone walkway. "I counted on your excitement. It never occurred to me that you would have replaced me."

Her perfect mouth was now devoid of any semblance of a smile and her sea green eyes turned stormy. "How silly of me, to have counted on a childhood promise after so many years."

Vlad glanced helplessly from Ioana to John, his tongue still tied in knots. Hunyadi, ever helpful, stepped behind his daughter. With his hand on her back, he stopped her escape. Or retreat.

"I do believe Vlad has something he would like to say to you. If he can remember how to put sounds together to make words sometime before the snow flies."

*When you were a child, you thought childish thoughts.*

"Ioana," he began.

*It is time to put away childish things.*

"I owe my life to you. Loving you, even though it was from

afar, it kept me alive." Vlad stepped toward her and offered both hands to her.

She did not take them.

Despite the ever-thickening lump in his throat, he continued.

"I wrote to your father the night I returned to Wallachia, asking for his permission to marry you and make you my own—words I planned to repeat to you tonight, as we knelt together in the chapel." Hands still outstretched, he smiled. "Why do you think I was in such a hurry to get there?"

Finally, Ioana placed both her hands in his and allowed herself to be pulled close to him. "And here I am, listening to a Gypsy woman named Mariela, who told me that we would be married the night you reclaimed your throne." A rose pink flush lit her cheeks. "She was so adamant, so convincing, that I have the chapel all ready for our wedding. It never occurred to me that you would have to think about it."

"Oh, I do and I have."

Ioana's eyes shot up from their downcast position to meet his.

Vlad stared down into the face of the only woman he had ever loved. "I thought about it daily, several times a day, every moment I was away from you. And I am thinking of it now. Ioana," Vlad lifted her hands to his lips. "Please, accompany me to the chapel and make this dream, this very dream right now, become real. Become my wife. Become my Voivoda." He brushed her fingers with a kiss before he dared look back into her face.

Tears shimmered in Ioana's eyes. Unable to contain her exuberance, she flung her arms about Vlad's neck. "There is nothing else I would rather be."

"I do believe a wedding is waiting for us," John said, a hint of jocularity in his strained voice. "You promised to make yourself my son-in-law, did you not? Afterwards, I shall ride straight to Transylvania to check on your mother." He dropped his voice low. "I heard Vladislav threaten your mother. I will ensure no harm comes to her, Vlad."

Vlad nodded his thanks to his natural ally.

Ioana squeezed his hand. "And you promised to make me your own, so long ago. Yet, you never asked me to wait for you."

He stroked her fingers with his thumb. Before he could open his mouth to tell her why, to tell her that he could not bear the thought of her with another man, that he could bear even less the thought of her unhappy or alone or loving a ghost, should he not make it out of Tokat Castle. As she had a keen ability to do, she answered for him, in words better than he could have made himself. "But how could I help but wait for you, when you are the one that God created for me to love?"

The chapel bell began to toll as Ioana slipped one of her arms in Vlad's and the other in her father's. "And I have thanked God more today than I have ever before in the entirety of my life," she continued, "for Our Father brought you home safe to me."

## Capitol Optsprezece

Targoviste Castle, Wallachia
in the Year of our Lord, 1448

*The traitor, Judas, had given them a prearranged signal: "You will know which one to arrest when I greet him with a kiss." So Judas came straight to Jesus. "Greetings, Rabbi!" he exclaimed and gave him the kiss. Jesus said, "My friend, go ahead and do what you have come for." Then the others grabbed Jesus and arrested him.*
*~Matthew 26:48–50*

Vlad stood at the bottom of the Throne Room and stared at the all-important seat that so many before, including himself, had fought, killed, and almost died for. The seat that belonged to the Voivode of Wallachia. Gypsies and Saxons alike lined the walls, some of them still wearing boyar blood from the battle the night before.

He glanced at his wife, Ioana. "My darling, pray do go and take your rightful seat, to the left of my throne, as Voivoda of Wallachia."

She nodded. "As you wish, Husband."

Vlad watched as she strode with such grace across the Throne Room. *Their* Throne Room. Applause rose from those in attendance. Once she had taken her seat, she nodded to him, a smile on her full, pink lips. He returned the nod before turning to face Roman Snagov.

With the memory of the night's battle fresh in his mind, Vlad spoke quietly. "And you, my most trusted compatriot. Do take your seat as my lead general, to the right of my throne."

Roman nodded and did as he was asked, to the tune of fresh applause from the victorious, yet rag-tag, army. Once he was seated, Mariela stepped forward and made a motion with her hand. Haunting music reverberated from the pipe organ, playing the notes that signified a royal entrance was about to commence. "Introducing, Vlad Drăculea III, Voivode of Wallachia and Defender of the Faith!"

Cheers and applause went before him as he made his way to his throne to the ancient tune reserved solely for royalty. His heart, banging in his chest as he made the royal walk across the Throne Room, beat with a combination of pride, humility, and a lifetime's worth of relief.

Once he was seated, the music squelched. The faces of everyone in attendance looked at him expectantly. Vlad wasted no time in attending to the most important business he could call to mind.

"Guards," he bellowed. "Bring in the remnants of the Ottoman soldiers, who came so generously and unexpectedly from south of the Danube to assist us to our ultimate victory against Vladislav the Pretender."

The guards did as they were commanded. Moments later, the white robed soldiers in their tall, white turbans who had not fallen in battle filed in. Nobody clapped or otherwise celebrated their arrival, but instead stood nervously.

From the corner of his eye, Vlad saw Roman's face turn to stone.

"Tell me, which amongst you is the leader?" Vlad's voice boomed in the Throne Room in a way it never had boomed before.

One of the Turks stepped forward and did a little bow. "It is I, Your Grace."

"What is your name?"

"Abdullah Aziz, Your Grace."

"Tell me then, Abdullah, who was it that dispatched you to Wallachia? And what is your purpose here in my country?"

Abdullah held his head high. "Sultan Mehmed II's favourite, Radu the Beautiful, dispatched us, unbeknownst to the Sultan, so that we might render aide against the pretender, Vladislav II, in helping you ascend to your rightful throne."

Vlad cocked his head. "Is that so?"

"It is, Your Grace."

Vlad sat in silence for a moment. "Since the Ottoman Empire, or should I say *one* member of the Ottoman Empire, saw fit to help our cause, I shall return the honor. My first order of business as Voivode of Wallachia shall benefit our neighbor to the south, since that neighbor saw fit to so selflessly benefit us." He adjusted on the throne to the tune of gasps from the crowd.

Something that resembled a smirk ghosted across Abdullah's face. "How kind. We are ever grateful for your generosity, Your Grace."

"In thanks for your selfless actions against Vladislav II, I cordially invite you to eat your fill and rest here at Targoviste Castle. At daybreak, my guards will dutifully escort you as far as the Danube. Carry with you this message, along with the pride of knowing that you did something noble in Wallachia."

"Humbly," Abdullah replied. "What, pray tell, is in this message of goodwill?"

"Royal Scribe?" Vlad glanced at Mariela. "Take this down."

Mariela retreated to a desk in the corner and prepared a quill and piece of parchment. When she was ready, she looked at Vlad and nodded.

"Greetings, Mehmed II. Be it known that, given the brave actions of the Ottomans in the defeat of Vladislav's forces on Wallachian soil, my first order of business as Voivode of Wallachia will be as follows."

He paused as Mariela scratched the words furiously across the parchment.

"In gratitude, I shall continue the long-held tradition of sending Wallachia's annual duty of ten thousand gold coins in the company of tributes, numbering no less than five hundred, to join your Janissary Army."

A deafening, uncomfortable silence filled the throne room as a smile played at the corner of Abdullah's mouth.

"Please expect Wallachia's annual tribute to arrive by month's end. In Christ, Vlad Drăculea III, Voivode of Wallachia."

Mariela finished the letter and folded it into thirds. "It is ready for your seal, Your Grace."

Vlad nodded. "Do seal it and hand it to Abdullah, Royal Scribe, so that the guards may escort them to the dining hall."

Mariela rushed through the deathly silent room to do as she was told.

Once the leering Ottomans had the letter in their possession, Vlad waved his hand dismissively.

The door scarcely closed behind them when Roman let loose with a roar. "You traitor! You played on my emotions to win me to your side—" He yanked his cutlass from its scabbard. "Only to betray me at the first turn! Damn you, Vlad Drăculea!" Roman pointed his cutlass at Vlad. "Damn you and the whole of the Draculesti line. I knew I should have sent you to hell on the tails of your father and brother."

The swooshing sound as the remaining guards pulled their swords filled the air. Each tip pointed at Roman's throat.

Roman's face was contorted in a mixture of agony and rage. "You may have fifteen swords pointed at my throat, Vlad Drăculea, but I have one pointed at yours. And one flick of my wrist would be all it takes to relieve a liar of his head."

Vlad held up his hand. "Guards, stand down. And do drop the wooden beam across the door. Nobody leaves. Nobody enters." He stared hard at Roman. "And I will thank you to sheath your cutlass, bite your tongue, and resume your seat."

Roman stood for a moment longer, his cutlass pointed at Vlad, suddenly unsure of himself. With everyone staring at him, he sheathed his blade and resumed his seat quietly.

Vlad glanced at him from the corner of his eye. "That will be the first and the last time you ever bark at me, Roman Snagov. If you cannot trust me, you are welcome to be relieved of your post as my general. The choice is yours. Make it now."

Roman shifted in his seat.

"Well?"

"I trust you, Your Grace." Roman studied his hands in his lap. "I beg you to forgive my outburst."

Vlad ignored him and addressed the whole of the room. "What I am about to tell you all must not leave this room." He motioned with wide sweeps of his arms for the entirety of his Gypsy and Saxon army to come in closer. "One must never trust the Ottoman Empire. Radu did not send the band of Ottoman soldiers, the Sultan did. They sided with us yesterday, because we were proving to be the victors. Had the battle taken another turn, they would have sided with Vladislav and given him the same story. I have heard it done hundreds of times during my years spent as a captive there."

He glanced at Roman. "You, General Snagov, will escort my five hundred Wallachian tributes to Sultan Mehmed." He paused, then smiled. "However, my Wallachian tributes will be like none they have ever received before. Five hundred armed men I will send. An army of volunteers, if you will."

Roman's face contorted from rage to confusion to relief.

"I just gave you your wish, you see." Vlad clapped him on the back. "You will lead this army straight to Tokat Castle, and thanks to my letter, the Ottoman spies that infect the countryside will relay your position the entirety of the way. There is always a party in the castle when new boys arrive. Rest assured, you will be welcomed with open arms and without a second thought."

Finally, Roman's face spread into a wide grin. "Do forgive me for doubting you."

Vlad was stoic. "You must trust me. I am not unpredictable in where my loyalties lie." He raised his voice so that all could hear. "My loyalty lies with God and Wallachia. I know I shall answer to

Him ultimately, and He entrusted me with all of you. I will not risk eternity for being a fickle traitor on earth. Nor should any of you. So, should you ever hear anything to the contrary about my motives or loyalties, you must know in your heart it is a lie."

The audience nodded and mumbled in acceptance.

"Now, please, go eat, drink, and make merry. You have earned it."

A raucous cheer went up from Vlad's court as the guards removed the wooden beam and opened the doors.

"Roman, Mariela. Do stay a moment, I beg you."

The old Gypsy and Vlad's top general did as they were asked.

Vlad kept his voice low. "Do either of you have any questions about the task at hand, how we are invading the Ottoman Empire in order to repatriate our Wallachian boys?"

Roman shook his head, then stopped. "How will I sneak men in as boys?"

Vlad's lips pulled up into a grin. "I am glad you asked." He turned to Mariela. "Might we be able to utilize your caravan for the cause?"

Mariela let go a guffaw. Her dark eyes twinkled. "The Sultan will not know what to think when our round-topped wagons cross his desert only to have an army pile out of them!"

Vlad glanced at Roman. "You are to oversee the gathering of volunteers for this mission. The men chosen should be strong, capable fighters. Because should they get caught—"

Roman nodded. "Say no more, Your Grace. I understand the gravity of this mission." He dropped his voice to a whisper. "I have been waiting for this my entire life. I will not fail you."

Vlad nodded.

Roman met his gaze. "And I will not come back without my son."

## About the Author

Sara Swann has authored more than thirty works of fiction and nonfiction to date. She holds her BA in History, her BS in Nursing, and is working toward her Masters of Science in Nursing Family Nurse Practitioner certification.

Sara lives with her family and their menagerie of rescue animals in Houston, Texas.

Visit Sara online at:
https://nursesarabooks.com/

## Also Available From

**WordCrafts Press**

*Idiot Farm*
Susie Maddox

*The Mirror Lies*
Sandy Brownlee

*Ill Gotten Gain*
Ralph E. Jarrells

*Pale Horse*
Michelle A. Sullivan

www.wordcrafts.net

Printed in Poland
by Amazon Fulfillment
Poland Sp. z o.o., Wrocław